JUNGLE FIRE

A Novel by BRUCE PORTERFIELD
Author of
Commandos for Christ
Twice Burned

BROWN GOLD PUBLICATIONS
Sanford, Florida 32771

. . . That the trial of your faith, being much more precious than the gold that perisheth, though it be tried with fire, might be found unto praise and honor and glory at the appearing of Jesus Christ . . .

I Peter 1:7

INTRODUCTION

The many instances in this book have been drawn from the experiences of many missionaries. Some of the heartaches, clashes of ideas concerning methods of mission boards, love affairs, raw jungle life in reaching savage tribes, the defeats and victories, have been the realities of many new and experienced servants of God.

Some of the methods and practices of a number of mission boards and their personnel are clearly seen in this novel. However, it is not the author's intention to single out any one organization while writing about some of the things that commonly occur.

The inward struggles and outward circumstances that Brian Allmand faces are the very things that many new missionaries have come up against. These or similar experiences have crushed and defeated many well intentioned missionaries because methods and principles became insurmountable barriers to them. Brian is one of the few missionaries with firm convictions who is willing to challenge what appears to be man-guided rules. He gets into all kinds of difficulties for speaking out on his convictions. Was it worth it? The results in principle of his convictions have also been those of a few in true life.

BRUCE PORTERFIELD

CHAPTER ONE

"Oh, God," Brian Allmand prayed desperately, "please keep Mr. Weatherton alive until I can reach him. I've got to make things right."

Brian twisted again in his jungle hammock. Menacing blackness enveloped him. Three feet of threatening swamp water waited below. Already four days in the murky swamp had made it impossible for him to cook hot meals. Just before he had crawled through the mosquito net into his hammock as the night was encompassing him, he had double-checked the knots to make sure he wouldn't get dumped into the water during the night. It had happened once before.

The young missionary checked his luminous watch. It was two A.M. Sleep hadn't come yet. He wondered how much longer he would have to slosh through the flooded jungle to reach the open grassland where the mission plane was reported to have crashed. Some relief had come to his heart when he had heard on the transistor radio that five days earlier an Army plane had spotted the wreckage and had seen someone waving. Who was it? The mission director, Mr. Weatherton? Or Mike the pilot? Did one of them get killed? Was there no other way to rescue them or did everything now depend upon him? Amidst the questions sleep finally came.

The gray Brazilian dawn forced its way through the tangled jungle. Squawking parrots were already heading for the palm-nut trees that usually edge the grasslands. With eyes still foggy from sleep Brian reached over to open the zipper that fastened the mosquito net to the hammock. Just then a movement startled him and he drew back his calloused hand.

"Oh, no," he groaned, running his fingers through his blond crew-cut. "Don't tell me I tied my hammock to a tree full of fire-ants!"

He looked again and could see thousands of red ants swarming over the outside of the hammock. He knew the fierceness of their sting. In the Viet Nam jungles, as an Army adviser, he had been stung by the merciless insects. For about an hour or so it had seemed as if they were stinging him repeatedly every few minutes. *Well named,* he thought. *Fire-ants.*

Brian lay still for several moments longer, wondering how he could get out of the hammock without being stung. A sigh of relief escaped his lips as he recalled gratefully that he had closed the net tightly when he had crawled into the hammock the night before. He had heard from the Brazilian nationals that several stings could make even the strongest man sick. Even though in Viet Nam he had been stung only a couple of times, he had felt as if his entire nervous system were aflame.

The broad-shouldered youth glanced at his packsack tied onto another tree. "Praise the Lord those pesky ants are not on that. If they were, I'd really be sunk."

Plans began to whirl through his mind when he saw that the ants could not be easily knocked loose. He checked to be sure his revolver was firmly secured to his belt. Where was a piece of string to tie the bottom of his trousers to prevent ants from crawling up? Then he remembered that inside the hammock was a small pocket containing string and an extra piece of net. Shortly the legs of his trousers were firmly tied. Carefully he tucked a box half full of raisins into his shirt. The empty half was evidence of what he had eaten for supper the night before. Taking a deep breath, he tore open the zipper of the hammock and rolled out. His hundred and eighty pounds of muscle and bone landed with a splash.

Staggering quickly to his feet with his blue shirt and levis clinging to him, he looked himself over to see if any of the threatening ants had latched on. Brian exhaled a sigh of relief as he found none. The sudden soaking was of no concern for in a matter of minutes the swamp water and perspiration would do the same. He surveyed the surrounding area.

The first orange rays of sun reached through the mist to touch a few moldy tree trunks jutting out of the dark water like sentinels. Brian looked back from where he had come the day before and saw the blazed trees. These blazes would be vital to finding his way back. "As good as any signpost on the highways back home," he thought as he pulled on the wet pair of tennis shoes he had taken from the pack. It was a bit difficult to put on the shoes under water.

Digging the machete out of his pack, he whacked it into a tree temporarily and then proceeded to put on the heavy pack. His face twisted with pain as the pack bounced on the soreness around the arrow scar that was still tender from the wound he had received six months before. The packsack strap had been rubbing the spot the previous day and had made it annoyingly sensitive.

No use taking any chances trying to roll up my hammock, he thought. *It's not worth it. If I can get out of the swamp today, I can get along without it. I did before during the Viet Nam fighting. With the Lord's help I can reach the plane today.*

The thought of Mr. Weatherton sent fiery pricks, like the stings of fire-ants, through Brian's mind. He had tried hard to patch up the differences between him and the mission director, but there were still injured feelings and misunderstandings. The threat of dismissal still hung ominously over him.

Several injustices had crushed him during the two and one-half years he had been in Brazil. And Mr. Weatherton had been the cause of many of them. Brian knew he shouldn't allow these bitter resentments in his heart. He must find the mission director and confess his ill feelings so he could once again experience peace in his own heart.

"Give me a chance to clean the slate with Mr. Weatherton," he prayed aloud as he took another compass-reading and prepared to slush through belt-deep water, swinging the machete to knock short slabs of bark off the trees. Now and then, as he struck a smaller tree, water came bouncing down from the leaves that had collected the heavy dew.

Thoughts continued to shoot through Brian's mind as the heavy pack cut into his raw shoulders. "Why should I risk my life for the man who has caused me so much anguish?" he growled. However, there was Mike the pilot. He was a welcome sight every time he flew to the tribe with supplies. Convinced that every life is a potential in God's hand, Brian knew he must do all he could to reach these two men.

"No doubt they're in desperate need of my help," he reasoned, with a sense of duty.

Now and then he stopped his weary plodding to wipe the sweat from his heavily tanned brow and to shift the pack. He reached into his shirt again and grabbed a few more raisins to dull the gnawing feeling that gripped his stomach. It had been five days since he had eaten a hot meal. Five days of plodding and fighting through the miserable swamp were fast draining away his strength. Already he had tightened his belt several notches. He was sure he was losing at least three pounds a day as a result of eating little and perspiring profusely from the tropical heat.

Brian glanced at his watch. It was seven-thirty, time for the morning radio contact. From the big side pocket of the packsack the husky missionary pulled out a small transistor radio wrapped in a plastic bag.

"CPX27N calling CPF95N. Are you on? Over." For a moment Brian felt helpless without a transmitter with which to call back, since this had been his duty back in camp.

"This is CPF95N. Good morning. What do you have to report? Over." Brian recognized the voice of Roy, his companion since language-school days.

"This is CPX27N. The latest news we have is that the Army plane flew over the crash area again yesterday afternoon to drop more food and medicine. The pilot reported having seen only one person. Apparently Brian and Irwin hadn't arrived yet. We're praying they might be able to make it in today. If you're listening on your transistor, Brian and Irwin, we dropped instructions to a . . . Mike—we think it's Mike—to keep shooting off signal rockets every hour, so when you reach the campo you'll be able to see where they are. Over to CPF95N."

"O.K., we got your message. Yesterday afternoon Irwin pulled in. About two days out Irwin wrenched his knee so had to hobble back in. He knew he couldn't make it through the swamp in that condition. Brian went on alone. If you hear me, Brian, we're really praying for you, buddy. Over to CPX27N."

Brian sighed deeply, his relief evident. "Thank You, Lord, for helping Irwin get back O.K."

Holding the leather radio strap in his teeth, he squirmed out of his packsack. It was pointless to haul the extra food and medicine now that more had been dropped to the men. After hanging the pack on a limb, he dug in and reluctantly dumped out some rice, salt, oatmeal and medicine.

"Well, Lord, under any other circumstances I don't think it would be right to throw away the things You've supplied, but I'm sure it's all right now to lighten my load so as to make better time.

14

I'm plenty bushed, too. I look to You to guide me the rest of the way . . ."

After buckling the packsack he struggled to put his arms through the straps. The lighter load was a relief. Glancing at his compass, he struck out again after he had taken another handful of raisins. The flooded jungle finally began to open as the sun hovered directly overhead. The water was only about a foot deep now. He fought on with thorns often tearing at his clothes. Because of the shorter trees, he was sure he was near the grassland. Carefully he shifted his gunbelt again. It felt as if it were cutting him in two. The pack continued to rub like sandpaper.

Before long, however, the jungle brightened as the trees thinned out. It was a matter of a few hundred yards and he would be on dry ground and the open campo. New energy raced through his veins as he pressed on. Since the Army pilot had reported that the plane had gone down about two miles south of the edge of the jungle, Brian felt his heart race with excitement and anticipation. Had he kept on a 170-degree course as he zigzagged for seven days through the jungle and swamp? If not, which way should he turn once he came upon the large open spaces?

Suddenly the jungle gave way to the wide, open, airy grassland. A puff of dense heat, with a thin, sour tang of mud, ruffled his hair as he slipped out of the pack. The brightness stabbed at his eyes. Cupping his hands over his tired eyes, he searched the wavy horizon for the orange smoke of a rocket. The minutes ticked away like hours and still there were no signs. His jaw dropped in disappointment.

"Lord," he breathed in desperation, looking heavenward, "which way should I go? There's no way to blaze a trail in this grass. Oh, God, what should I do?"

As the sun began to lean heavily toward the west, Brian felt desperately alone, heavily burdened physically and spiritually. The vastness of the campo before him and the jungle behind was like the jaws of a vise pressing him in its grip. Jungle and grasslands knew no mercies toward intruders.

The smoldering animosity between Brian and Mr. Weatherton had started shortly after he and his friend Roy Clark had arrived together at the mission base in Brazil to begin language study. That had been more than two years ago. It seemed that new, fresh ideas and zeal had soon clashed with archaic methods and thinking.

CHAPTER TWO

"Hey, Roy, it's Saturday morning. What do you say we go down to the open market after breakfast and pass out some tracts?" Brian spoke enthusiastically as his safety razor cleared another path down his youthful tanned face.

"Sounds like it might be a good idea," Roy replied, crawling out from beneath his mosquito net. "Anything for a diversion from this grueling language study. Think we should check with Mr. Weatherton to see if it's O.K. with him?"

"Why bother the director?" Brian retorted, feeling pressure rising in the veins of his neck. "Aren't we down here to reach these souls with the Gospel message?"

"Yeah, I agree, buddy, but we've been down here three months, and I haven't seen any of the missionaries do any of that and they haven't held any street meetings either. I was wondering if there might be some reason for it." Roy raised up from the bed to stretch his tall lanky frame.

Brian frowned into the mirror as he finished shaving. "I wonder if one of the mission boards has claimed that territory. Yet the few times we've been over to the market I haven't seen anyone down there witnessing or selling Bibles. These people have got to be reached."

"I know," Roy replied, pulling his T-shirt over his head. "But I've got the impression that Mr. Weatherton wants to know our every move. I suppose things have happened in the past that have marred the testimony of our mission so he feels he has to be very cautious with new missionaries."

Brian could see Roy was as cautious with his words as a diplomat. He had often wished that in the past he had been more careful about what he had said. Yet, he reasoned, if a man has convictions or he sees things that are not right, how is he going to get his thoughts across if he doesn't speak up plainly? Brian's few conversations with the mission director, Mr. Weatherton, had shown him that there would surely be difficulties in the future, for often their ideas and methods did not coincide.

"If you ask me," Brian began, slamming his fist into his other hand, "I think . . . " He stopped suddenly, drawing in his lips. Conviction was etched across his wide forehead.

"You think what?"

Dropping his gaze, Brian replied. "I'm sorry, Roy. I was going to say something about Mr. Weatherton. Then I realized I shouldn't run anyone down. He's doing his best, I'm sure, with a sincere heart."

Just then a small bell clanged, indicating that it was five minutes before breakfast. Roy slipped out of the room as Brian finished scraping off the shaving soap. After-shave lotion scented the plain room. Clothes hung loosely from a bar suspended in the corner. A closet would be useless as the lack of air would cause everything to mildew. A couple of uncluttered dresser drawers, made by local carpenters, filled part of the room. Against one of the light blue walls was a large table at which both missionaries studied in the evening with the aid of a hissing pressure lamp.

Both men had just finished making their beds and were rolling up their mosquito nets when the second bell rang.

Several tables in the spacious dining room were empty. The Weathertons and their three children were seated at one table, the printer and his wife and four children, at another. Mike the pilot, his wife and son, another young married couple and Brian and Roy occupied the third table.

Mr. Weatherton moved toward the half-wall where there was more light for reading. The top half of the wall was screened to the tile roof. With a large Bible in his hand, the dignified director began to read a Psalm. Soon he was interrupted by the entrance of his attractive and energetic daughter, June. Brian could feel excitement surge through his veins as he watched her hurriedly take her place at the table. Her flowing brunette hair gently touched her crisp white blouse.

Brian felt a jab in his ribs. "Come back to earth, buddy," Roy whispered with a wide grin that spread nearly from ear to ear. Brian flushed as he realized his buddy had caught him staring at June, who always seemed so full of life.

Just the week before, she had returned from the States with an R.N. degree. She had been doing secretarial work for her father

17

before coming to the general hospital for six months of studying tropical medicine.

When she had joined the language students at the volley-ball game the day before, Brian had suffered a sound ribbing from Roy for making more goofs in the game that day than during the entire three months previous.

"She's quite an attraction," Brian had admitted when he and Roy were showering after the game.

As Brian's face cooled he could hear Mr. Weatherton reading from the Bible. He looked saintly, with tinges of gray edging his hairline. Brian wondered how he could wear a black tie and white shirt all day long. He glanced at his own T-shirt and for a moment felt out of place. Yet Roy and Mike the pilot were wearing T-shirts too, and looked more comfortable. It was the accepted custom at the mission base and language school. On the street, however, the missionaries wore ties and shirts like most nationals, and often Roy heard Brian say, "Get on your hangman's noose and shirt and let's take off for town."

The director finished reading and took off his heavy-rimmed glasses to make a few comments. His dark brown eyes blazed with authority and when he spoke, his voice was crisp and firm. Now and then, however, lines of kindness deepened around his mouth as he smiled. A well-upholstered chin showed he had been away from the rigors of the jungle trail for several years.

Brian chanced a quick look at the other table and June flashed a pleasant smile in return. Mr. Weatherton finished praying and the maids brought in the oatmeal, toast and coffee.

Getting up from the table after breakfast, Brian put his hands on Roy's shoulder. "Well, buddy, have you made up your mind about going with me to the market to pass out a few tracts and maybe sell a Bible or two?"

Roy looked down as if to search for words. He was a bit taller than Brian. Although fifteen pounds lighter than his friend, he was every bit as strong and agile, as Brian had discovered in a few friendly tussles.

"Don't think I'll go today, friend," Roy said, looking up with troubled brown eyes.

Brian stopped his slow pace across the patio toward their room and stood directly in front of Roy. "You want to go, don't you? But you're afraid you might get in Dutch."

"Guess you're right," Roy sighed heavily, his hands shoved down into his pockets.

"Tell you what. Let's go and talk it over with Weatherton and see what he says. Are you game?" Brian asked with hope in his tone.

The two started to walk slowly again to get away from the sun that had crept over the red roof and began to beat into the patio. "Yeah, I'm game," Roy drawled falteringly.

The director's office was off to the side of the large, spacious living room that was separated from the dining room by bookcases about the same height as the half-walls. Large eaves outside protected the open, airy rooms from both rain and sun.

After knocking and being invited in, the young missionaries sat on the cushioned wicker chairs before the dark mahogany desk. Old books, spotted with mold, lined the walls on two sides, and the morning coolness filtered through the screened walls that also admitted the light freely.

Mr. Weatherton leaned back in the old swivel chair, placing his glasses on the uncluttered desk. "What do you fellows have on your minds?" he asked sedately. Roy looked to Brian to lead the way.

"We've talked over the fact that if we don't get out and witness, or pass out tracts or sell a few Bibles, we're liable to dry up spiritually," Brian began, sitting on the edge of the chair. "Our Portuguese isn't anything to brag about yet, but we feel we need to start using what we've learned."

"I'm glad to hear of your interest," Mr. Weatherton began seriously. "What do you men propose to do?"

"I've been down to the open market a few times and have felt burdened about the fact that there's no one selling Bibles or passing out tracts. With people coming in from the country it's a tremendous opportunity." Brian realized he was tense and made an effort to relax. "Do you have any thoughts to the contrary about our going over to the market today?"

The director shifted his weight as his face clouded. "Well, it's like this. We haven't done anything like that in the market because the Brazilian Interior Mission claims that territory. Their church is just a couple of blocks away from the market."

"Claims that territory!" Brian retorted. "Don't tell me South America is like Africa, where missions claim certain territories and they don't have enough missionaries to reach all of the people, yet holler their heads off if someone else walks across the line. What about the souls that are going to hell? I . . ."

"Just a minute, Mr. Allmand," the elderly man began sternly.

"We have worked in harmony with other mission boards for many years, and we don't intend to cause trouble by intruding upon their territory."

Brian felt indignation well up inside him. "True, Mr. Weatherton, I don't believe we should proselyte, but when another mission board is doing nothing to reach the people on their own doorsteps, then I think it is only fair to allow someone else to work the area. I have no objections to sending new believers to their church, if they choose. I understand it's a sound mission. The main thing is to win the unsaved to Christ before it's too late."

"I agree we are here to win the lost," Mr. Weatherton cut in as he leaned forward, folding his arms on his desk. "But this is no time to break mission etiquette."

"You mean it is more important to uphold etiquette than to snatch these souls from a Christless eternity?" Brian asked, his eyes flashing.

The director looked coldly toward the young missionary. "You'll understand in due time. You're new on the field, and, like most new missionaries, you're full of zeal but still lack wisdom and tact. Our methods have been proven over the years, and we don't intend for any untried fresh-from-college chap to tell us what or how things should be done."

"I can see why some mission boards haven't grown much over the years," Brian snapped back. "Others are growing rapidly and doing tremendous things because they have taken advantage of new ideas and methods and they don't downgrade the zeal and vision of young men."

"Mr. Allmand, I . . ." The director flushed and started to rise.

"I'm sorry, Mr. Weatherton. I realize I'm wrong in getting hot under the collar. I apologize. My convictions are the same; nevertheless I realize I was wrong in allowing my emotions to rise to the surface."

There was a moment of tense silence. Brian was deeply disturbed by the restrictions. He wondered if he should have been more diplomatic and cool. Wouldn't the gospel message have spread much faster in past years if there hadn't been this problem of mission etiquette? He was beginning to see why their own mission board had made little progress throughout the years.

"Do you have any suggestions, Mr. Weatherton, as to what we might do?" Brian asked, staring at the small, threadbare carpet on the smooth cement floor.

"Well, let me see," the director began, jutting his chin and squinting as if in deep thought. "There are a couple of our believers who are sick and you could visit and encourage them. Come to think of it, you wouldn't be able to help much because of the language barrier."

There were a few more lame suggestions before the historic meeting was over. Archaic ideas and methods had clashed with a desire to reach souls for Christ. Brian was becoming more keenly aware of the barriers and hindrances and disappointments that already threatened to chill his enthusiasm. The prospects of a bright missionary career began to cloud.

Somehow, Brian realized, the situation wasn't as Mr. Weatherton had pictured it when he had spoken in his church several months before. The young man had received the impression that the heathen, in their desperation, were constantly begging the missionaries to come to their homes or villages to tell them about Jesus. The message had been well presented and certainly challenging and appealing. In fact, Brian had put his last five dollars into the offering plate that was passed after the message. Inspired to the core, he had discussed with Mr. Weatherton, after the meeting, the possibilities and requirements for service with the mission.

Now the situation was quite different. Brian's hope of reaching the fierce Panube tribe farther north was threatened by mission-board fences and a tradition-bound mission director. Both Brian and Roy had talked to Mr. Weatherton about starting a work among the tribes. The response had been anything but encouraging, but at least he had agreed to discuss the matter with the field council and to investigate the possibilities. Brian had been shocked when he first learned that his mission had no work among the Indians, since its name included the word "Indian."

Brian and Roy walked slowly across the patio once again. The sun was already reaching new heights and was pouring its fierce rays upon the mission compound beside the great Amazon River. Brian's heart was heavy as he spoke dejectedly to Roy.

"Guess maybe we, or I should say I, got my wings clipped."

"Don't let it shake you, buddy." Roy spoke softly with sympathy in his voice. "The Lord knows, and I'm sure He'll work things out."

"Yeah, I know. But that doesn't relieve the burden to witness for the Lord today. What do you say we have a little prayer meeting now, and then I'd like to go uptown on my bike and pick up a couple of things."

Soon they were in their room again and on their knees, expressing their hearts' desires before the Lord.

Just before dinner, Brian came back from town and, bursting into the room, exclaimed with eyes sparkling, "Hey, Roy, I got something to tell you!" As his eyes became accustomed to the shaded room he could see why no one answered. The room was empty. After a shower he continued his humming as he quick-stepped to the living room to wait for the dinner bell. As he opened the screen door he suddenly felt as if all the blood were being drained from his body. Before him sat June and Roy humped over a game on the coffee table.

"Howdy, Brian, come join us," Roy said sheepishly as Brian stumbled to the table. "I heard you singing on the way over. Sure different than a couple of hours ago. What goes?" Brian quickly composed himself after a sudden twinge of jealousy.

"Pull up a chair," June beamed. "While we're waiting for dinner we thought we'd start a game of Scrabble. Three will make it more interesting."

"We're in for a licking if this brain plays," Roy added kiddingly.

"Aw, come on, buddy, lay off," Brian said with a lingering glance toward June. As he pulled up a chair beside the coffee table to join the game, he continued jokingly, yet with hidden meaning, "If June has as many brains as looks, I think we're both sunk, Roy."

June's round face flushed but she was quick to retort in the same mood. "If you gentlemen don't behave, I'll have you on the carpet before my father."

Roy sat up straight and looked at Brian. When their eyes met they both burst out laughing. "Tell her, Brian, what happened this morning."

"Naw, let her guess."

"Come on, you guys, what's so funny?" June asked, her sparkling eyes dancing from one to the other.

After a bit more teasing, Brian said softly, cupping his hands to his mouth, "Your father already had us on the carpet this morning. We learned we're just plain green, ignorant missionaries. Have pity on us and put in a good word for us."

While June was working on her turn at the game, Roy looked up and asked, "Anything new uptown?"

"I'm praising the Lord for the opportunity I had to talk to a

22

couple of college students about the Lord. Both knew English. They were real interested and invited me over tonight for a Bible study. Tremendous opportunity." Brian's face shone with excitement.

The days slowly became weeks, and Brian was getting a firm grasp of the Portuguese language. The Saturday-night Bible-study group had grown to approximately twenty young people. Brian usually spoke in English and one of the college students translated. Some were won to the Lord during the meetings and others were led to Christ through the witnessing of the nationals. Brian usually took three or four fellows out to the country to witness on Saturdays also. This was the highlight of each week. Soon, however, the joyous experience, for which Brian had praised the Lord, became another heartache. He had noticed for several days that the atmosphere seemed electrified. Then came the inevitable summons that Brian had expected—a call to the director's office.

"Where you headin' for? You look kinda solemn," Roy said, running his fingers over his crew-cut as Brian headed for the door.

"Mr. Weatherton wants to talk to me," he returned glumly.

Pity shadowed Roy's countenance as he dabbed at a razor nick on his prominent cheekbone. "Are you in Dutch again?"

"Beats me, pal. I wouldn't be surprised if I broke some goofy rule I don't know about." Brian hesitated at the door. "You might remember me in prayer, buddy."

"O.K., happy landings," Roy said as he watched Brian saunter across the patio.

As the young missionary sat before Mr. Weatherton he was reminded of the time he and his fellow officers in Viet Nam had gotten a real chewing-out from the three-star general. Rigid Army life had taught him to take orders unquestioningly, whether they were just or not. He had envisioned missionary work, however, to be characterized by teamwork and co-operation. Before coming to the field he had met several missionaries who had told him that their missions operated in this way. They did not believe that only one man knew the will of God for every life, but that His will was often ascertained through the Spirit-guided discussions and decisions of the entire group.

The quick succession of thoughts screeched to a halt when Mr. Weatherton began to speak. Brian looked up and once again the elderly man removed his heavy-rimmed glasses.

"Mr. Allmand, I hear you are having Bible-study classes on Saturday night. Is that not so?"

Thinking that before discussing the main reason for the interview the director would talk about something on which they both agreed, Brian sat back in the wicker chair to relax.

"Right. I've certainly been praising the Lord for the souls saved. You've no doubt noticed that some of the young people have come to our Sunday services."

Mr. Weatherton's piercing dark eyes stared for a moment toward Brian's feet. "I don't begrudge the fact that some souls were saved. You're to be commended on that."

There was a moment of silence as the older missionary seemed to wrestle with his thoughts.

"Nothing wrong with that, is there?" Brian pleaded.

Weatherton raised his stare and bore in on the young missionary. "It looks to me as if I have a real problem on my hands in that because of your disobedience and insubordination our mission is in ill repute again."

"I don't get you. Where have I been disobedient or broken any mission rules? If you're referring to my Bible class, I feel every step I've taken has been the Lord's leading."

"Lord's leading!" Mr. Weatherton exploded. "Do you think, young man, that God would lead you to start a Bible class without my permission and without checking to see if you are infringing on another mission's territory? Besides, the director of the Brazilian Interior Mission complained about the intrusion."

"As I see it, Mr. Weatherton, the Lord led me to speak to a couple of college students who were in the same store I was. I could see the Word of God was getting through to them. They invited me over to their room to discuss this further. That first Saturday evening they came to know the Lord Jesus Christ as their personal Saviour. They wanted their friends to hear, too, so we agreed to meet the following Saturday. The group has been growing ever since. If this is God's leading—and I think I'm mature enough to discern it—and you call it disobedience and insubordination, I frankly don't understand how you can feel that way."

Brian could see the director's neck veins bulging, and he was sure another tongue-lashing would be forthcoming. He was fully aware of the battle within his own heart to subdue rising resentment and anger.

"Listen, Mr. Allmand," the heavy man began stormily. "I . . ." His words stopped as if his mind had gone suddenly blank. Then he began with a different thought. "Mr. Gates, our assistant director, you know, is due in tomorrow. Now that language school will be over next week, there is a possibility we might work something out for you, Roy, and Mr. Gates to make preparations to reach the Panube tribe."

Brian was speechless for a moment. The opportunity to attempt a friendly contact with the savages took him by surprise. As nothing had been said for months, he had wondered if the whole idea of starting tribal work had been scuttled. Did Mr. Weatherton decide on it to get him away from the town where his presence was causing trouble and embarrassment?

"What about the Bible-study class? Who will take over?" Brian heard himself asking.

"That will be taken care of," the director replied sternly. "I want you to understand now that if you don't prove yourself out in the jungle, you'll be a man without a mission board."

The words stung Brian to the core. Later, as he limped wearily out of the office, he realized the cost of being aggressive for the Lord. Would part of the price be eventual dismissal?

CHAPTER THREE

Brian and Roy met with Irwin Gates to discuss the proposed trip deep into the interior. Their conversation began with reminiscences and a couple of the current political jokes. Brian was sure Mr. Weatherton had discussed the present situation with Irwin. He could detect a reserved coolness in the senior missionary, in spite of his effort to be cordial. As the men sat in the living room a cool breeze filtered in. It was heavy and jungle-scented.

The hissing pressure kerosene lantern hung by a wire from the rafters. Two other lamps lit the adjoining dining room where a handful of children had their schoolwork spread out before them. June leaned over one of the students as she gave needed assistance. How helpful and considerate she had been when there had been a need, Brian had noticed. He tried hard to keep from glancing her way, for should he get caught, he knew Roy would rib him for it.

Brian studied Irwin's heavily bearded yet close-shaven face. His square jaws were counterbalanced by an abundance of wavy hair. His matter-of-fact conversational tone was not the result of his own experiences but reflected what he had learned from others. He had the obvious air of a senior missionary, and Brian was sure he would not be allowed to forget it. Was Irwin a puppet of Mr. Weatherton or did he have spiritual convictions that sprung from a close walk with God? Brian's silent questions ceased as he heard Irwin ask, "Tell me about your experiences in Viet Nam."

"I learned quite a bit about life in the jungle and how to survive against its threats. I guess you know it respects no man who intrudes. I'm sure some of the things I experienced will come in handy here in the Brazilian jungles."

Conversation was pleasant as Brian and Irwin, who had been a medical corpsman in the South Pacific during the Second World War, compared notes. Yet the situation seemed strange. In the

Army, Brian had held a higher rank than Irwin. Now, on the mission field, Irwin had the authority, as assistant director, to give orders.

A bell rang, indicating it was time for the younger children to head for their evening snack. June went out with them, and Brian's heart flipped as she smiled at him. With an effort he brought his thoughts back to the serious planning.

"What do you think, Irwin, of digging up a couple of more men?" Brian asked carefully as he sought the opinion of the middle-aged man with bits of gray fringing his hairline.

Irwin rubbed his bushy hand over his jaw and blocked chin to give himself an extra moment to ponder the question. "What do you have in mind?" he began with a Texas drawl. "The three of us can handle the task without any difficulty."

"Sure, as far as the work of traveling upriver and clearing jungle to set up camp is concerned, the three of us can handle it. What I was thinking of was to have a couple of more men as added protection in case the savages have any evil intentions."

Irwin rolled up his white shirt sleeves, exposing an old Army tattoo. "Well, you have to consider that the Lord is with us and He'll see to it that the savages won't carry out any intentions to harm or kill. Takes faith, you know. Hope you've got it and won't let us down in a pinch."

"I've got faith, all right," Brian assured him, undaunted by Irwin's authoritative manner. "Faith is practical and allows no presumptuousness."

"Even if one man went out to contact this tribe, the Lord would be faithful to protect," Irwin emphasized.

"I'm not doubting even for one minute God's power and ability to protect. Nevertheless if we don't spend time in prayer to be in a condition to hear His guiding voice, then whatever choices are made in the flesh are bound to be disastrous."

"Isn't your attitude a little out of tune?" Irwin jabbed.

"I don't think so," Brian said with hurt in his voice.

Then, looking over to Roy, who had been silent, Brian hoped his friend's conviction would be like his own. "What do you think, Roy?" he asked.

Roy leaned forward, resting his arms on his knees. "I really can't say."

Brian breathed deeply as lines of disgust edged the corners of his mouth. "Just like Roy," he thought. "He doesn't want to hurt anyone's feelings by taking sides."

Looking again at Irwin, Brian asked, "Do you have any particular reason for believing it would be a hindrance to have five men on this expedition?"

"Frankly, I don't feel it's practical to temporarily pull a couple of more men from their area of work and I don't see how it will add to our protection. It's just reasoning in the flesh, and not complete faith and trust in the Lord." Irwin shifted his weight in the squeaky chair.

Brian paused for a moment in deep thought. Should he drop the subject and go along with Irwin? If he did, would he be carelessly committing his life to the ideas and whims of another man? Would God overrule if Irwin was wrong and the savages did attack? Brian had considered the cost of contact work in the past. He had heard about others who in the past two decades had been killed by savages, and he was not afraid to die for the Lord. Yet life was precious because of the potentiality of being an instrument in God's hand, of taking the Gospel to those who had never heard.

"It's like this," Brian began slowly. "In the Army when you had to give commands you didn't go by your feelings. You had to consider the safety of your men as you took into consideration what the enemy thought and how he worked. Sure, we had superior firepower, but some of the enemy's tactics got us into some real trouble."

Brian looked up as he smelled coffee brewing. It was near evening snack time. Then he continued. "Sure, we've got terrific firepower, the power of God. Yet, we're going to be fighting a crafty enemy, the powers of darkness. Scripture says that one shall chase a thousand and two shall put ten thousand to flight. There must be a principle involved that should not be taken lightly."

"I believe you've got something there," Irwin said thoughtfully as he also turned his head in the direction from which the coffee aroma was coming. "I'll talk it over with Mr. Weatherton and see what he thinks."

Brian could see in Irwin a desire to be co-operative, but past experience had so molded and enslaved him that he carried out the director's wishes unquestionably. It seemed like a chain reaction—Irwin giving in continually to Mr. Weatherton and now Roy giving in to Irwin. Was this the basis of and way to unity? Would he disrupt this chain reaction and cause disunity on the field? Didn't the Holy Spirit bring about unity by moving upon hearts so that each missionary sought the best for his fellow worker?

Shouldn't there be a co-operative exchange of ideas until the entire group agreed upon the next logical Spirit-guided step? These thoughts flashed back and forth across the horizon of his mind until a tiny bell in the kitchen announced snack time.

Through the following week preparations were made and supplies were purchased for the ten-day trip upriver, and for an additional four months. By that time an airstrip could be made and further necessities flown in.

The day before the trip was to begin, the fellows' room, strewn with supplies and equipment, looked as if a tornado had hit it. Brian was oiling his shotgun when Irwin walked in.

"Howdy, fellas, I . . ." Irwin stopped suddenly, his eyes flashing on the gun. "Were you planning to take *that?*"

"Sure, why not? I'd like to sink my teeth into some of those wild turkeys and tapirs I've heard about. Who knows, we might tangle up with a tiger or a big snake."

"The savages must not see us with guns. They'd likely fill us full of arrows right on the spot and our contact would be forever lost." Irwin walked slowly toward a packed box, raised one foot upon it and leaned forward, resting his folded arms on his knees.

"Might be a good idea if they saw us carrying guns," Brian responded. "It just might cause them to think twice before pulling on the bowstring or hurling a lance." Brian could feel the tension building up like an electrical charge and braced himself for a verbal explosion.

Irwin stood up straight, his eyes narrowing to a slit. "You mean you'd kill an Indian if you were in a tight spot?"

"I didn't say that!" Brian shot back. "I wouldn't kill an Indian under any circumstance. If things got rough, I might shoot in the air to scare them off."

"You're trusting again in the strength of the flesh," Irwin accused with suspicion in his voice. "Don't you think God is able to protect us in any circumstance?"

"Sure," Brian spoke assuringly, opening his fingers wide to emphasize his point. "But I'm sure God expects faith to be practical. Jesus never condemned the disciples for carrying swords. It's true, Peter got in trouble for using his sword at the wrong time for the wrong purpose, but, nevertheless, he'd been carrying it right along."

Brian knew by reading missionary books that a few tribes had respected the white man more without guns. The Lord had led very clearly in this action. However, in many cases that he read about or heard of, the Indians withheld from killing because they saw guns. He had strong leanings in this direction. Was this the way in which God was expressing His will for this tribe? His thoughts were drawn short as Irwin spoke.

"This is an entirely different thing," Irwin retorted. "We'll leave the guns behind."

"Listen, Irwin," Brian began pleadingly, "I hate to disagree with you, for I want us to have good fellowship and unity on this trip. We've got to have the blessing of the Lord. Yet our lives may be at stake because of a foolish move. I . . ."

"Right," Irwin interrupted. "Taking guns is a foolish idea, if you ask me, and it'll jeopardize our lives all the more."

Brian felt resentment, like the pressure of hot steam, building up within him. "If you ask me, we're in for real trouble. First you and Mr. Weatherton think it's needless to have five men. Now you refuse to take guns. It's not right to expose our lives foolishly." Brian realized how tense Irwin was and noticed that the tone of his own voice was sharp. Conviction gripped his heart.

"I'm sorry, Irwin," he began, hurt stinging his eyes. "I'm sorry I allowed myself to get heated up to the point where I blew my safety valve."

Irwin wilted momentarily. He opened his mouth to say something but no words came. After a moment he turned to Roy, who hadn't said a word.

"What's your opinion, Roy, about taking guns along?"

"Well," Roy began with hesitancy, "I rather go along with Irwin's ideas. Then, too, Brian has some good points to consider."

There was a long silence. Deep thoughts filled Brian's mind— thoughts that involved life or death, success or failure, hell or heaven for immortal souls involved, the end or beginning of the fulfillment of his burning desire to reach tribes for Christ. A continuing clash of ideas could ruin his hopes.

Finally he broke the silence. "Where do we go from here?"

"Let's go talk it over with Mr. Weatherton," Irwin suggested, pointing his thumb toward the office door.

Brian took a deep breath. "I don't want to get into an argument with him; my survival cord is frazzled down to a thread. There seems to be little choice. I guess I'll leave my shotgun here so there'll be peace in the family."

Irwin shifted his weight and, with hands on his hips, began, "Well, fellas, that's real progress, and I'm pleased this item is settled. What do you say we leave at the crack of dawn?"

"Good enough," Roy said, getting up to stretch. I've got the gas and oil ready. The barrels are down at the river in Don Juan's shack."

Shortly after Irwin left, Roy glanced over at Brian, who was still seated with his chin in his cupped hands. "Penny for your thoughts," Roy asked carefully.

Brian disgustedly slammed one fist into the palm of the other. "I wish I were like you."

"How's that?" Roy's mouth remained open, half in surprise and half in wonder.

"You're easygoing. Nothing seems to bother you so there's no clashing of ideas. My convictions are constantly getting me into trouble. If they were minor things, there wouldn't be any difficulty in giving in. Yet, when our lives and the failure or success of a work are involved, I somehow just have to speak up. I surely would have appreciated it if Irwin had taken my suggestion that we spend some time in prayer together about this expedition. What do you say we have a time of prayer before the Lord right now?"

After the two had risen from their knees, Brian started to pack the articles he had laid out on the bed. He then walked thoughtfully to the dresser and reached into the top drawer, only to withdraw his hand empty. He stood a few moments, then turned to Roy. "What would you think if I took my revolver?"

Roy spun around, eyes wide and brows lifted. "You'd probably end up cooking your goose."

"I know. Yet I can't shake the feeling I should take it along. When we're in Indian territory, I could keep it under my belt and shirt. The savages wouldn't see it. It wouldn't trespass Irwin's concept as to what might happen if the savages saw a gun, for they wouldn't see this one. Then, too, he knows I wouldn't shoot to kill."

"Yeah, I guess you're right as far as that thinking goes. But what if he finds out?" Roy's voice was nearly a hush.

"I'll be careful so he won't, but if he does see it, we'll just let the chips fall where they will. I wouldn't be surprised but what we might need it. Do you have any qualms about my taking it?"

"Well . . . I guess not," Roy returned, with hesitancy in his voice. "I just hate to see you and Irwin clash again. It would only lead to another pow-wow with Mr. Weatherton. I enjoy working with you, buddy, and I'd hate to see you get dismissed from the mission."

Brian, his arms folded, continued to lean on the dresser, staring into the open drawer. "You don't know what it means to me to be here on the mission field and soon to be on our way to contact a savage tribe. It's terrific. But, then, it's wrong to be careless. Well . . . here goes." With that Brian drew out the revolver, slid it inside a pair of work socks, and shoved it down to the bottom of the packsack.

Immediately Brian felt a burden lifted from his heart. Could this feeling of relief be the indication of God's leading and confirmation? Or was this deceptive and therefore wrong? Brian was scarcely aware of his packing as a debate raged within his own heart. Was taking a revolver worth the possibility of disgraceful dismissal from the mission? He reached to the bottom of the pack where it lay snugly. His entire future could be changed by this small object. Now was the time to take it out of his pack or else accept the possibility that it might change the course of his life. In the past, decisions in the physical realm had been easy to make in comparison with the spiritual dilemma he was facing now.

Looking up with determination in his eyes, he shoved the revolver a bit deeper into the pack and sighed with relief.

The following morning the sky was laden with heavy gray and blue clouds. Everyone was up early. Mike the pilot assured the three men that he was looking forward to the time when he could serve them by bringing in supplies and flying them in and out, which he would do as soon as possible. He told them that if it was too difficult or too time-consuming to make an airstrip, they should notify him by mission radio and he would fasten on the pontoons and land on the river. "Only thing is," he apologized, "I can carry only two hundred kilos instead of the usual three hundred."

Even Mr. Weatherton was on hand and in a good mood. Brian was thrilled as the small group gathered in the patio just before leaving and the director prayed for their safety and for success in the work. Wearing blue jeans and shirts, the men looked like typical jungle travelers as they headed down toward the shore. Their helmets were painted white with blue stripes and their machetes, dangling from their sides, were also painted blue and white.

There was a reason for this color combination. The gift axes and knives and cans were similar in color. If gifts were scattered widely along the Indian trails or on sandbars and then found, the

Indians would associate these gifts with the men who had axes and knives similar in color to theirs. In years past, nationals had put out "gifts" on the edge of their little farms and when the Indians had cautiously approached, they had been shot down in cold blood. Such happenings in the past had made it more difficult to make friendly contacts, as Brian had learned by reading missionary classics. Perhaps along the way they could talk to farmers to see if anything similar had happened to the Panube tribe.

Glancing once again at the lowering sky, Brian carefully checked the tarp that was tied down over the boxes and bags of cargo in the middle of the dugout canoe. Irwin took his position at the outboard motor and Roy took his place in the front to be on the lookout. Every time the gas tank needed refilling they would take turns at the motor and lookout.

Soon the motor was gurgling and muttering as it warmed up, and the last-minute good-bys were given. Brian felt a needle pierce his heart as they pulled away from the shore where June also was standing and smiling. Was she dabbing at a tear? For him? For Roy? Brian had certainly enjoyed the few times they had relaxed together over a game or simply chitchatted.

Soon the heavily laden dugout canoe was knifing its way through the mighty chocolate-colored Amazon. Out in the middle, where the current was surging faster, mighty tree trunks were bobbing and turning. Passing islands of grass and lily pads, the canoe glided gracefully on its long journey toward the Atlantic. As the boat slowly fought its way, hugging the shoreline, Brian reviewed past events.

The past was as somber as the overcast sky and as turbulent as the waters below him. But there was one thin slit of light in the dark clouds of his past. That ray of hope was the promises of God. Then, too—maybe June.

CHAPTER FOUR

The days passed slowly under the blazing tropical sun. About every three hours the men changed positions when the gas tank had to be refilled. The blond hair on Brian's arm stood out in contrast against the darkening skin. Clean clothes lay drying over the baggage as the heavily laden canoe ploughed the mighty river that had narrowed with each day. The fifth day the small party of men reached the mouth of a clear black tributary.

"Hey, look at the difference!" Roy shouted to Brian above the noise of the motor. "What'll you have? Chocolate milk?" He pointed to the left. "Or root beer?" He pointed to the right.

Brian dipped his cup into the fresh black water and was amazed to find it as clear as glass. It was the first time he had been able to see the bottom of his cup since they had left the base.

"Why is it so black-looking and yet so clear?" Roy asked with a puzzled look.

"I suppose it has the same explanation as they gave me in Viet Nam," Brian offered. "Jungle vegetation causes it. The water doesn't come from the mountains where it tears away the subsoil."

The varied green jungle, with billowy clouds crowning its massive head, reflected upon the smooth water, and for a moment Brian had the sensation of flying over the exotic scenery.

Irwin, nestled in a comfortable position between the two piles of supplies, glanced up from writing in his diary. The space in the middle of the dugout canoe afforded a place to bail out the water. Where large nails had been bent over, the wood was rotten and water continually oozed in slowly. One time the canoe, riding only six inches above the waterline, had tipped when it had struck a submerged log, and he had been forced to bail frantically as several gallons of water had rushed in.

Other than that there had been little excitement as the men traveled day after day, often stopping at small farms to give out tracts and New Testaments. Brian enjoyed the outdoor life and sitting around the campfire an hour or so before crawling into his jungle hammock. Since it was the dry season, the mosquitoes were not numerous. The first couple of nights he had waited for Irwin to take the initiative in leading devotions. But he had not done so.

Brian wondered why he, being the leader of the expedition, had not assumed this responsibility. Was he so preoccupied that he didn't think of it? Was he spiritually indifferent because he continually yielded to Mr. Weatherton? Or was this spiritual apathy caused by the fact that many of the mission principles were not Scriptural? Therefore, the third night, as the three sat around the sputtering flames, Brian had pulled out his New Testament and said he would like to read a passage that had been a real blessing to him during the day. Irwin had said something about making it short as he was tired and wanted to hit the sack.

Now, as he looked back on those evenings in the pitch-black jungle, he began to get a deeper understanding of the men with whom he was working. Brian reflected on Viet Nam, where the presence of danger, of the lurking Communists seeking to penetrate their lines of defense, had drawn the men closer together. Even though many were ungodly men they had been deeply concerned about the well-being of their fellow men. Brian had expected that the co-operation and fellowship among missionaries would be much deeper and satisfying.

His expectations had not been realized, although the conditions were similar. Here, he reasoned, the powers of darkness would be seeking ways to attack and destroy their fellowship with each other and their confidence and trust in the Lord. There were already subtle temptations to pamper the flesh, to think of one's own interests. He was sure that eventually the enemy would try to cause physical harm or the loss of this expedition. Was it possible that the others didn't sense the reality of spiritual warfare? Did the concerns of this life dull their awareness of a real spiritual enemy? Could methods, preconceived ideas, or presumptuous faith lead them to believe that their real enemy was only a paper tiger?

Brian longed for deep fellowship, for oneness in thinking. True, things had gone smoothly during their times of discussion around the campfire. Perhaps this was because of a deliberate attempt to be cautious, to avoid discussion of anything controversial. He believed that where there was true fellowship it was not necessary to weigh every word or wonder about the true meaning behind a remark.

Screaming white and gray birds with red beaks and legs interrupted Brian's thoughts. Up ahead Roy ducked as one came careening in.

"I guess they're protesting our invasion of their territory," Brian said with a chuckle. "They're sure mad."

The sea-gull-like birds circled and swooped again and again as the throaty gurgle of the motor continued to push the missionaries deeper into the interior. Now and then turtles slithered off moss-covered logs and large fish could be seen in the shallow water along the beaches. Tall jungle now replaced the low, thick taquara (similar to bamboo) brush that lined the Amazon banks.

Here and there a path led up the bank to a small hut where rubber workers tapped the wild trees. They usually worked the trees only during the dry season.

After eight days of traveling, the men found that the black river had narrowed considerably. The rubber workers' camps were more scattered. Figuring they were nearing the edge of civilization, and that the Brazilians dared not go farther to work, the three fellows agreed to pull into one of the small thatched huts that hugged the embankment. Heavy smoke was blanketing its way through the jungle and rolling over the bank to hover over the river like smog in a big city.

A dark-skinned, sad-faced woman appeared at the high bank with two small children, clad only in shirts, clinging to her colorless dress.

"Good afternoon, señora," Brian said as they climbed up. "Is your husband around?"

"Good afternoon, señores," she responded with a raspy masculine voice after heaving a stick at the two threatening dogs. "No, he is out collecting rubber milk. Won't be back until about sundown."

Brian looked at his watch. It was eleven-thirty A.M. He moved forward a bit to put his hands on the little children's heads and offer them pieces of hard candy, but they hid behind their barefooted mother. She finally persuaded them to take the candy.

"Tell me, señora," Brian began, keeping his eyes on the skinny dogs still snarling a short distance away, "are there any more rubber workers farther upriver?"

"Used to be three others but they were abandoned last year," she responded as she walked over and shoved a couple of burning sticks beneath a pot of rice boiling over the fire outside the hut.

Roy and Irwin drew up close to the fire beside Brian, and Irwin asked with excitement in his voice, "Why did they leave?"

"Savages," the heavy woman replied as she lifted the lid of the black kettle to look at the rice.

The men looked at each other with raised eyebrows and Irwin spoke again. "What happened? Did the savages attack?"

"In each of the places the Indians put arrows in the paths of the rubber workers. In two camps the people had enough sense to take the warning and got out the very next day. The rice is about done. Won't you stay for dinner?"

"We don't want to inconvenience you, señora," Brian said apologetically.

She begged them to stay and the fellows agreed to do so. Then Irwin went back to the subject. "What happened at the third place?"

"Well, Don Miguel, that's who it was, said no Indians were going to drive him out. He'd shoot 'em down if he saw one." She checked the pot of beans on the far end of the stick that straddled the fire.

"Yes, then what?" Irwin asked, his dark eyes widening like a boy watching a western on television.

"Well, one day his woman got worried because he didn't show up by nightfall. She took the lamp and went down the trail. Before she went very far she was horrified to find her man dead with five arrows in his back. Then she grabbed his gun and ran back to the house. Within a few minutes she loaded up the canoe with her three children and paddled the rest of the night to get to us."

"Have the Indians been around here?" Brian asked as he moved over and sat down on a large ball of smoked rubber.

"Don't think so. At least they haven't put any arrows on the path," the dark-skinned woman answered as her children still stayed close to her. "The dogs were doing a lot of fussin' the other night. Might have been an animal close by. We just got back a month ago. The only thing suspicious was that we found some of our rubber cups missing that we had hid."

"Sounds like we're in for an interesting time." Roy spoke for the first time. Brian glanced over to Irwin, who seemed a little pale.

"I've got only two plates and two spoons. Do you men mind bringing up your plates from the boat?" she asked, apologizing.

"I'll get 'em," Brian said as he took off down the bank. After digging out the utensils, he looked up to see if anyone was looking. Then he burrowed down to the bottom of his pack and pulled out his revolver and holster, and after looking around again, he drew in his stomach and slipped the holster under his belt. Then he pulled out his shirt tail to cover the evidence.

"Who knows, it might come in handy," Brian mumbled as he crawled over the cargo to get to the front end of the canoe and then scrambled up the embankment with the utensils.

As the Brazilian woman heaped the men's plates she asked, "What brings you gringos up this way? Are you looking for gold or diamonds?"

Brian waited a moment for Irwin to speak, for he knew more Portuguese, although he had a worse accent. Irwin seemed to be deep in thought as he shoveled in his rice and beans. Then Brian began.

"No, we're missionaries. We've come to make a friendly contact with these Indians with the purpose in mind of telling them about Jesus Christ, God's Son. Of course it will take a few years to learn their language so we can explain to them that Jesus died on the cross and shed His blood so that they might have eternal life, too."

He dipped his spoon in again and the woman asked, "Oh, you must be Protestants. Bah! Why risk your lives? These savages are just animals." With that statement, made disgustedly, she spit on the ground. "Ave Maria, protect us from these savages," she said, looking up and crossing herself.

Brian pulled out a tract and asked her if she could read, explaining that this contained the plan of salvation.

"No, I can't read. My husband can," she returned. "But we are not allowed to read anything from Protestants." After that statement she excused herself and went over to the hut to add more wood to the smoking fire which was used to smoke rubber milk onto the ball of rubber. Brian put the tract back into his pocket.

Irwin commented. "Doesn't look like you'll get very far witnessing to her."

The men finished eating and washed their plates and spoons down at the river. The woman continued to busy herself turning the ball of crude rubber over a small hole in the ground from which hot smoke was pouring. As she turned the ball she slowly added more rubber milk that was already nearly coagulated. The missionaries thanked her for the meal and said they would be on their way.

It was Brian's turn at the motor as the canoe twisted its way up the river. Now and then a log protruded from the middle of the black river, disturbing the mirrorlike surface. He could see that Irwin wasn't reading now but was searching the banks of the river with his piercing eyes. Roy was sitting on a box in the front of the canoe. As the sun began to sink heavily toward the west, Brian hugged closer to shore in the shadow of the towering trees draped by hanging vines.

He thought the motor was making much more noise than usual. He listened again but it was humming smoothly, and he realized he was a little tense. If the savages were hunting in the area, the motor would expose the intrusion of the white men prematurely. Perhaps that was the reason he thought the sound of the motor seemed unusually loud—like a careless crook stomping into a house instead of tiptoeing.

Late in the afternoon one of the abandoned huts of the rubber workers came into view. When Brian eased the canoe toward the shore, he could see that three feet of brush had grown up around the small clearing.

"Might as well camp here for the night," Irwin said as he got up to stretch. "It'll be a good place to talk things over and plan our strategy."

"I'm all for it. But as soon as we do a little clearing, what do you say we take a dip before starting supper?" Roy asked as he tied the boat to a sapling.

While Irwin and Roy cleared away some of the jungle growth, Brian refilled the tank and laid the motor inside the canoe to check the gearcase for grease. After putting the motor back in place, he carried up some of the necessary cargo.

The rice began to cook over the fire when the men walked a short way upriver to the sandbar to bathe. The sun was low and the tree tops caught the last rays. Brian walked slowly up the sandbar before getting ready to swim. Suddenly he felt himself freeze in his tracks. His breath was gone. Right in front of him were footprints.

He breathed slowly, and it seemed as if once again he was suddenly being dropped onto the battlefield by a helicopter. It was the same feeling he had experienced in Viet Nam—the feeling of being watched by the enemy waiting to pounce upon him. In the jungles on the other side of the world it had been his objective to bring outward peace: now his purpose was to bring the Gospel message that gives peace within. Nevertheless, before the objectives would be accomplished there would surely be difficulties, spiritual warfare and—he tried to erase the thought from his mind —perhaps casualties.

He shook himself from his ominous thoughts and gave a sharp whistle. The other men looked up to see him motioning for them to come.

"What's the matter?" Roy asked, water flattening the hair on his chest.

"Look down here." Brian pointed to the sand. For a moment both Irwin and Roy stared with mouths open, and then their eyes followed the tracks to the edge of the jungle.

"Can you beat that!" Irwin exclaimed, rubbing his hand over the back of his neck. "I sure didn't think we'd run across the savages this soon."

Brian could see goose pimples all over Irwin as he said, "I didn't either, for in most contacts I've read about, it took two to three years. What's your next move, Irwin?"

"Guess maybe we'd better hurry and finish bathing and eating and talk over our plans and tactics."

"I wonder if one of those savages was on this sandbar, and when he heard our motor in the distance, he took off like a scared rabbit," Roy added as the men went back to where they had left their clothes.

Brian wished he had his revolver with him. It was back in the packsack where he put it just before coming to the beach.

Little was said as the inexperienced missionaries ate their supper. Brian was sure the others were deep in thought just as he was. Were they suddenly feeling helpless in the territory of hundreds or thousands of fierce warriors? Would Irwin's reckless faith hold up under these circumstances where the men were completely defenseless? Could he, Brian, possibly be wrong in believing Irwin's faith was extreme? Would precisely that kind of faith be required to protect them? Somehow he couldn't escape the conviction that they should have five men with guns. True, he reasoned, as he took another bite of food, even five men with guns would be useless if a horde of savages attacked. Nevertheless, the Lord might use the shot of a gun into the air to save their lives and to win their enemies' respect eventually.

Night settled upon the small group of missionaries as they sat on a log finishing their meal. Deep-throated frogs had begun their nightly chorus. Already the men's shadows were silhouetted like huge giants against the black jungle wall as the flames of the fire fingered heavenward. Close by was the small, abandoned thatched hut just big enough for three hammocks. There were bamboo walls on three sides and a crudely made bamboo bed was in one corner.

Finally Irwin broke the silence. "I wouldn't be surprised if we're not too far from the Indians' village and right in the middle of their hunting grounds. It looks like we've reached our destination."

Brian poked at the fire with a small stick as Irwin continued with an air of authority. "I think we'll stay here and attempt a friendly contact. If we've been seen already by the savages, it shouldn't be too long before we meet them. That'll at least save us a lot of trail-cutting and hunting for their trails to leave gifts."

"Isn't this the place where the Brazilian was killed?" Roy asked, staring into the fire. "If I understood the woman right, there is one more abandoned rubber camp farther up. Might be worth-while to take a look at that."

Brian swatted a mosquito and then got up to stand beside the fire. "I was thinking the same thing. Would the savages think we've come here to avenge the man they killed? If we were at the other place, they might not think that way."

"Nonsense!" Irwin spoke with disgust in his voice. "It doesn't make much difference what they think, for the Lord will protect us. Doesn't the Word say His angels have charge over us?"

Brian checked his shirt tail to make sure it was covering his revolver. He knew it would be useless to argue this point, for it would only cause friction. Surely this was the time they needed to be united and in complete harmony. Putting this thought aside, Brian brought up another subject.

"I suggest the first thing we do tomorrow is clear more of this underbrush away, at least a couple of acres. That way we can see what's going on. I suggest we clear far enough back, say the distance an arrow could travel. Then we could put up a log cabin."

"Why a log cabin?" Irwin questioned with a bit of irritation in his voice. "We've got a tent to put up."

"I know," Brian said, wondering if they would lock horns again. "What I had in mind was to build a small log cabin for protection in case of an attack."

Irwin sighed deeply. Brian could see that he was disgusted. Then the older man inhaled deeply as if to speak, but he merely bit his lower lip. Brian was sure that Irwin had restrained a rebuke in an effort to maintain harmony. Then he shifted his weight on the log and spoke.

"Let's clear a good section of this underbrush tomorrow. That'll take at least a day. Then we'll see what the next step should be. Maybe we can hang up a few gifts, too."

"Sounds good to me," Roy agreed, stretching his legs. "What do you say we all hit the sack?" Irwin got up and stood opposite Brian.

"Before we do let's read a bit from the Word and have a time of prayer together." After Brian spoke, he looked to Irwin for approval. He sensed that the leader resented his taking the leadership in spiritual matters. He wanted the assistant director to do so, but since he didn't, Brian took the initiative, for he was convinced that prayer and fellowship were vitally important.

Brian turned to the Twenty-third Psalm, which he thought was appropriate for this time. Knowing it from memory, he scarcely looked at the pages. He paused a moment after the verse, "Yea, though I walk through the valley of the shadow of death, I will fear no evil: for thou art with me . . ." Then he went on, pausing once again after he had finished. "Surely goodness and mercy shall follow me . . .?"

While he lay wide awake in his hammock that night, he could hear both Roy and Irwin turning in their hammocks now and then. No doubt they were wide awake too, thinking. Finally Brian's eyes became heavy and he felt his heart slowing to a normal pace. Soon sleep overcame the plans and counterplans that had raced through his mind.

The jungle became alive with many birdcalls announcing a new day. Brian slipped out of his hammock and dug in the ashes, hunting for hot coals. Soon a fire was going and water was heating for oatmeal. He went down to the canoe and brought up the box that contained the radio and transmitter and another that held a battery. Before long he had the aerial strung between a couple of trees and was ready to check in with the home base when seven-thirty came.

When the oatmeal ceased to boil freely, Brian set it aside and yelled, "Hit the deck, men. Chow is on."

"Aw, come on, buddy. Don't be a wet blanket," Roy mumbled kiddingly.

42

"Here come the savages," Brian said with a smile.

"What!" exclaimed Irwin, bolting out of his hammock. "Where?"

Brian roared with laughter. "I knew that would get you out of the sack."

"I don't think that's very proper," Irwin grumbled as he rubbed his eyes. "This is no place for joking."

Brian watched him as he brushed the dirt from his feet and put on his shoes and socks. "If you ask me, it's the best place to have humor. It breaks the tension and, at times, the monotony. Of course, we haven't gotten to the monotony part of it yet. Let's eat."

Shortly after breakfast it was time to talk to the base. Brian described the trip and asked those at the various outposts to pray for them as the savages were close by. Then Mike the pilot came on.

"This is CPX27N calling CPF95N. Howdy, Brian. Sure good to hear from you after all these days. I just heard the report that the savages are around. Here are a couple of suggestions so let me know what you think. First, let's go on every day at 10-12-2-4 and 6 so as to check for your safety. If we don't hear from you in three successive checkout times, I'll be in with the plane. Second, check the river for logs and see if there is a stretch long enough for taking off. Over."

"This is CPF95N. O.K., Mike. I agree with you on the hours of checkout. The river is good just below us for landing but I'll check again for snags. Over."

"O.K., I suggest you pull your canoe part way up the sand bar and put a red shirt or something beside it so in case I have to come in I'll be able to fly along the river and pick your place out. Do you have anything else? Over."

Brian checked to see if the other men had anything to say. "We'll be back on at ten o'clock. Irwin says he sends his love and greetings to his family. That's all we have. Over."

"O.K. Who do you send your love to? Over." Brian could hear Mike chuckle just before he stopped transmitting.

"Knock it off, buddy. Out and clear from CPF95N." Brian smiled. He thought, "I'd sure like to send my love to June, but things aren't that far along."

The missionaries worked hard all day, clearing the jungle but leaving the larger trees standing for shade. On the three trails that went out from camp to the wild rubber trees, the fellows hung up steel axes as gifts to the savages. There was no difficulty getting to sleep the second night as everyone was dog-tired.

Again at the crack of dawn Brian was the first one awake. As he waited for the cereal to cook he dug into the Word of God for promises and encouragement for the day. He felt uneasy. Was this because Irwin's principles of operation exposed them to unnecessary danger with no protection? Or was he really carrying out, of necessity, Mr. Weatherton's instructions?

When the oatmeal was cooked, Brian set it to one side and glanced over to see if Irwin and Roy were stirring. There was no movement so he decided to let them sleep. Brian walked slowly over the area that had been cleared the day before. The smell reminded him of the freshly cut alfalfa in Nebraska. The rising sun was crowning the tops of the trees with orange splendor. "Beautiful Lord," he prayed as he stood looking heavenward, "I enjoy being out here beholding the works of Your hands. Father, I'm grateful You are here to guide and direct. I pray . . ."

Moments passed as Brian talked with the One whom he loved and to whom he had dedicated his life. A stirring in the distant brush brought him back to earth and his surroundings. Was it an animal? A savage? He lifted his shirt tail and his hands rested upon the hidden gun. Suddenly he feared that he was too close to the edge of the thick brush. The savages could easily shoot from a hidden position.

Suddenly he noticed that the ax which had been hung on the trail was gone. His heart tried to jump out of his chest and his blood ran cold. What was this thing hanging where the ax had once hung? Cautiously he crept forward. A dead rattlesnake— its mouth propped open with a stick! An arrow, too! Stuck right in the middle of the trail!

Brian spun around and hurried back to the hut, glancing over his shoulder every few seconds. "Hey, men, get up! The axes are gone!" There was a stirring in both hammocks.

"I hope you're not joking again." Roy groaned as he peered through the mosquito net.

"No, I'm not! The axes are really gone!"

"You sure?" Irwin demanded.

"Come out and see for yourself. And, besides, they left a dead rattlesnake and an arrow."

"Doesn't sound too good, does it?" Irwin gasped as he hurriedly dressed.

Roy was right on Irwin's heels as they rushed to where the snake and arrow were. After a quick glance they both hurried back to the hut at the edge of the river. Both looked pale, as if they had seen a ghost. "Somehow," Brian reasoned, "Irwin's looks and actions just didn't match his dogmatic proclamation that everything will work out well." He felt sympathy well up within and wondered if there wasn't some way he could have a heart-to-heart talk with the assistant director.

"Guess maybe we got our evacuation orders," Brian said as he dished out the porridge. "I wonder how many days they'll give us."

"This is the logical place to make a friendly contact so as far as I'm concerned, we don't move," Irwin said emphatically. "I believe the Lord led us here and that He will soften the hearts of the savages right away so we can make a friendly contact."

Roy looked up at Brian, expecting him to say something in answer to what Irwin had just said. Brian smiled and patted his shirt where the revolver was concealed, and Roy gave a quick wink of acknowledgment.

Brian studied Irwin a moment. Were his bold words merely covering his fears? He seemed like a man not sure of himself, a man who had to talk confidently to bolster his own spirit. Brian's heart again went out to the leader. He could sense his desire to be companionable and to treat the other men as equals, but he was also struggling to perform his duty—fulfilling Mr. Weatherton's wishes and constantly reminding others of who "ruled the roost." Brian's heart swelled with compassion for the enslaved assistant director. "I don't think Irwin's convictions are genuine. I must help him. But how?" he wondered.

"What's your plan for the day?" Brian asked Irwin as he scooped in another spoonful of cereal. There was silence.

"Oh, huh? Did you say something to me?"

"Yeah. I asked what your plans were for the day." Brian was slightly annoyed. Why couldn't they discuss the situation freely and come to a majority decision? Wouldn't it be wonderful if all three were of the same mind? An error could easily be made when one man made all the decisions.

Irwin slowly sipped his coffee, apparently stalling for time. Then he answered, "I don't know. Maybe it would be best to sit around all day and wait for the savages to come out. Or maybe we could go down the rubber trail a ways and scout around."

45

Brian's face clouded as he spoke with conviction. "I don't mind sitting around but I think it would be foolish to go running around on the rubber trails. We could do plenty around here, such as making a table and bench and some shelves out of split palm or even bamboo."

"Sounds like a good idea to make the place a little more livable," Irwin agreed.

From time to time the men checked the clearing for further signs of the Indians. Other gifts of beads and knives were put out. Brian checked in at the regular seven-thirty A.M. radio time and the even-hours during the day. Mike assured them he was on stand-by alert. During the day all were busy making various articles. It was four o'clock, time for the emergency radio skit. Brian was just inside the hut warming up the radio. Irwin was outside splitting some bamboo for the table Roy was beginning to put together just inside the hut.

"This is CPF95N calling CPX27N. Are you on, Mike? Over. Just a minute. Hold on. It sounds like some savages are yelling. Just a minute, I'll take a look." He went outside. Before him, on all three sides, were light-brown naked savages with chests and faces painted red and black. How fierce they looked as they crouched and danced close to the edge of the clearing! Some were making gestures as if to throw their spears while others readied their bows and arrows. Then suddenly they charged forward. As Brian dashed back to the radio he heard Irwin shout, "Let's hit for the river."

Brian pressed the microphone button. "Mike! Mayday! Mayday! Here comes the whole bunch of them with spears and bows and arrows. I . . ." Brian dropped the mike to dash for the river.

"Your gun, Brian!" Roy shouted as he started out just behind Brian.

"Look out, Irwin!" Brian shouted as he reached the edge of the embankment. Just then a savage flashed by swinging his lance, hitting Irwin on the head and knocking him unconscious. The savage ran off. Brian dashed to grab Irwin and drag him down to the river so that he could take the injured man across to the other side. Just as he was about to reach him he saw another savage close by drawing back on his bowstring to shoot at Irwin as he lay on the ground with a bleeding head. Brian leaped to cover Irwin's body. Just as he landed on top of him he felt the arrow pierce his own body. Roy dashed for the two men as other naked savages drew close to shoot. Brian could feel Roy fumbling under his shirt. *My gun,* Brian thought as he started to raise himself. Then he felt his gun being torn loose from the holster. Roy blasted several shots into the air. Brian looked up to see the savages fleeing into the jungle, leaving their weapons behind.

"Good boy, Roy. You saved the day," Brian said with real effort as his face tightened in pain. He coughed as he rose from shielding Irwin. He spit blood.

"Hold on a minute, buddy. Let me get this arrow out of you," Roy said tenderly, tucking the revolver into his belt.

"Wait a minute. Let's break it off and leave the rest in for now," Brian said painfully as his buddy helped him into the hut. "If we pull it out, I'll no doubt bleed all the more. I forgot Mike is still standing by on the radio. Give him a call."

Brian glanced over to Irwin, who was on his hands and knees and shaking his head as he regained consciousness.

"Are you still on, Mike? Over." Roy said excitedly into the microphone.

"I'm still here. What happened? Is everyone O.K.? Over."

Roy gave a report of what had happened. Then he added, "Can you make it in yet today? Brian has an arrow deep into his side. It must have pierced his lung as he's spitting blood. Bring in a few quarts of plasma and about three shots of morphine. We have enough bandages and antibiotics. Over."

"Just a minute," Mike answered. There was a minute of silence. Roy rushed over to help Irwin into the hut. Mike came back on. "I figure it will be a two-hour flight. We have three and a half hours of daylight yet. I'll try and get the pontoons on within an hour and try to make it. Build a big fire and make lots of smoke. Also be on the stand-by the rest of the day. Over."

"O.K., bring in two or three men if you can. Standing by."

Roy quickly inspected Irwin's head. The skin was broken open and there was a good-sized lump. At the same time Irwin became unconscious again.

"I think he'll be O.K.," Roy said reassuringly. "First I'll get the syringe on to boil so I can give you a shot of penicillin and a shot of blood coagulant. Then we'll cut that arrow off and patch you up."

Roy started the fire and put on a kettle to boil. Then he dug into the supplies for the medicine.

"Where's my revolver, Roy?" Brian asked, wrinkling his face in pain.

"Under my belt. Want it now?"

"That's all right. Hang on to it. I . . ." There was a gurgle in Brian's throat as blood nearly choked him. Roy rushed over to help him into a sitting position. His throat cleared. "It might be best for now not to say anything about my jumping on Irwin to protect him and about your shooting into the air."

"O.K., whatever you say," Roy replied as he made Brian more comfortable.

"Better reload the gun. In the side pocket of my pack you'll find some shells."

Shortly Irwin revived. Feeling the lump on his head, he asked with a blank look. "What hit me? The last I remember, a bunch of savages were yelling and heading our way. I was just getting ready to head for the river. Then . . . I don't remember any more. Where's Brian?"

"Behind you over by the wall with an arrow in his side," Roy answered as he prepared the syringe. "One savage came up from behind you and clobbered you with the side of his lance. If it had been an inch lower, you'd have been scalped."

Irwin turned to see Brian, who looked pale. "Sorry they got you. They must have hit and then ran. The Lord must have driven them off before we all got killed. Are you all right, Roy?"

"Yeah, I'm all right. We certainly were fortunate the Lord undertook for us all. Brian got the worse of it, but we'll get him off at the crack of dawn to where they'll fix him up in good shape. Mike hopes to get in before dark. O.K., Brian, I'm all set to fix you up, buddy."

As Roy headed over he stopped suddenly for a moment. Brian lay motionless. He laid the syringe back in the pan. "Give me a hand, Irwin. He must have been bleeding more than I realized. Let's get his head lower than his body. He's probably going into shock."

Roy moved quickly as his experiences in the Korean War had taught him to do. He cut off the arrow and then, after snipping off Brian's shirt, he put compresses around the stub of an arrow sticking out of his side. Would the plane make it in before dark with the desperately needed plasma?

CHAPTER FIVE

The sun began to slip over the horizon. Irwin had already fully recovered and his head was partly shaved and bandaged. Both he and Roy were tossing green branches on the huge fire to increase the volume of smoke that curled its way upward. The little plane had left two hours before, and every fifteen minutes Mike reported his position to his wife, who was standing by at the base. Then Mike's voice came in again. "Panube camp, Panube camp, Roy, do you have that fire going? I don't have much daylight left and I can't spot your smoke. Over."

"This is Roy. Yeah, we got a good fire going and lots of smoke going up through the trees. May the Lord help you to get in before dark. Brian is serious. Over."

"O.K., I can fly another fifteen minutes and if I don't spot you, I'll have to land on the first lake or river I can find. Standing by."

Roy checked Brian's pulse again. It was still weak but unchanged from when he had checked a few minutes before.

"Panube camp, I spotted your smoke. Pray I'll make it before it's too dark. Over."

"Praise the Lord!" Roy shouted, tears filling his eyes.

In about ten minutes, as the sky deepened its red glow, Mike swooped over the tree tops. The white plane was like an angel winging to the rescue. The men could hear the pontoons touch the water, then the decelerating of the motor. Both rushed down the slope with flashlights for by the time the plane taxied up to the port it would be difficult to see. Soon the plane came around the curve and drew up to shore.

"Howdy, men," Mike's voice was husky with emotion as he stepped out on the pontoon. "It sure was nip and tuck getting here." He threw the rope and Irwin grabbed it to tie the plane to a tree.

"Wow, sure good to see you, pal!" Roy returned, and the two hugged each other as they stood on the large pontoons. "We were sure sweating it out."

"Guess we'd better hurry and get out the medicine. I brought Dick and Jim along." Mike fastened the door open as he spoke. "I'm sure you know these men."

After the brief greetings everyone hurried to the hut. Roy quickly set up the apparatus to give Brian an intravenous. Mike suggested that meanwhile they have a prayer meeting and ask God to spare the injured missionary's life and restore him to health.

Within an hour Brian was conscious again and his pulse had returned to normal. When he opened his heavy eyelids he recognized the men. Weakly he spoke. "Hi, Mike, Jim, Dick. You guys sure are a sight for sore eyes."

Mike squeezed his massive hand. "We're pulling for you, buddy, and at the crack of dawn we'll be on our way."

Brian smiled faintly. "How's Irwin?"

"I'm right here. Roy has me all patched up."

Both Dick and Jim, who were second-termers on the field, pitched in and prepared packaged soup to go with the hamburgers and pie they had brought.

Brian was comforted to see all the men in camp. The morphine shot had deadened the pain and he felt like getting up. Roy cautioned him to lie still as even the tiniest movement would make the bleeding worse. Brian heard the others talking, as they sat around the blazing fire, about the recent happenings and about taking turns to stand guard during the night.

"Hey, Roy," he whispered softly, "how are they going to stand guard with no guns?"

Roy leaned close after checking the bottle of plasma that was nearly empty. "They're loaded, buddy, armed to the teeth."

Brian whispered softly through his teeth. "Too bad we didn't have the extra men and guns before. What did Irwin say?"

"Not a word yet," Roy replied in a low voice.

Brian heard Jim say he'd stand guard the first three hours, Mike took the second watch and Dick the third. The night was quiet and Brian thought it strange that the frogs weren't gurgling out their bass tunes. Could something be disturbing them? Could the savages still be lurking near?

Jungle hammocks were hung in a triangle near the fire. Brian had been slipped onto an air mattress so that he would be more comfortable, and a cot net had been hung over him. He noticed that Irwin was writing a letter. Was he sending a report to Mr. Weatherton? What does he think of me now? The sleeping pill soon took effect and he drifted restlessly off to sleep. He didn't know a thing until he heard Dick waking up everyone as the dawn began to push the jungle darkness away. The aroma of coffee was as refreshing as the first warm winds of spring.

Mike flipped the switch of the transmitter to warm up the radio so he could get a weather check. The voice over the radio said that the weather was fine at the base and that arrangements had been made for an emergency operation at eight-thirty A.M. at the hospital. Mike said take-off time would be about six A.M.

Soon Brian was lifted gently, carried down to the river and put into the plane. He wanted to walk but Roy would not hear of it. "I'll be back as soon as they let me," Brian told Roy. "Thanks loads for your help, buddy."

The next few hours were hazy in Brian's memory. He remembered that there were people lifting and carrying him, and he had vague recollections of white gowns and overhead lights and odd smells. Later in the day his mind began to uncloud.

"Where am I?" he asked as his heavy eyelids raised slowly and he stared at the ceiling.

"You're in a hospital room," a feminine voice beside him answered softly. "You're going to be all right. The doctors did a good job patching you up."

"Oh," Brian mumbled as he slipped back into sleep from the effects of the ether. Then a few minutes later he turned his head toward the nurse and spoke with a thick tongue. "Who was that speaking to me?"

"This is June," she said in a soft voice, putting her hand on his forehead. "I was assigned to be your special nurse. We're going to pull you through."

"June. Oh." A weak smile crossed Brian's face but he couldn't lift the weights that seemed to hold his eyelids down. "How nice."

Tenderly she put her hand over his wide wrist to take his pulse once again and after a moment she wrote something on a chart. His other arm was strapped down and a long tube was dripping life into his veins from a suspended bottle. His massive chest heaved and lowered rhythmically as he slept once again. In the middle of the afternoon he opened his blue eyes wide, clearly free from the effects of the ether.

"Hi, June," he said with a contented grin. "I never dreamed I'd see you here beside me. Did you just get here?"

She chuckled lightly. "I've been here ever since they wheeled you into the operating room with the broken arrow sticking out of your ribs. You spoke to me a while back but I guess you were still doped."

Brian sighed deeply and grimaced in pain. "Aye, feels like the doctors left their knives inside. What's the scoop?"

"One lung was punctured and collapsed and the tip of the arrow also went into your stomach. We can praise the Lord those savages don't use poison on their arrows or you'd be a handsome dead duck."

Brian could see concern etched in the corners of her sparkling eyes. She continued. "When you came on the radio at four o'clock yesterday and said the savages were attacking and then suddenly you went off, Mike sent word around. Everyone dropped what they were doing and we all dashed over to the living room and listened to my transistor. It seemed like hours before Roy came back on, but I guess it was about fifteen minutes. We were sure praying."

"Thanks, kid. I'm sure the Lord undertook for us," Brian returned, laying his hand by his side. June put her hand over his. He started to withdraw but her cool hand felt good. He sensed that the gesture had meaning. Something akin to a thrill tingled every nerve.

"Where's your dad?" he asked casually.

"He'll be back from Rio de Janeiro in a couple of days. Some sort of mission business, I guess." June tucked a couple of strands of brunette hair up under her nurse's cap. "How are you and he getting along?"

Brian rubbed his hand over his crew-cut and arched his eyebrows. "That's a good question. No doubt in a couple of days we'll know. I don't think I've proved myself according to some of the old-fashioned mission thinking."

"How's that?" June asked with sadness showing in her eyes and in the lines around her youthful mouth.

"There are continual clashes between what I call presumptuous faith and practical faith."

"What do you mean?"

52

He grimaced again when pain shot through him as he tried to shift his position. June stood to help him adjust his pillow. "Well, its like this. Presumptuous faith says God is able to protect under any circumstances and that therefore it is sinful to trust in precautions such as having extra men and carrying guns. Practical faith trusts in the Lord all right, for without Him we can do nothing. Yet it will not be careless and take chances."

June looked down at him, studying his face. His heart was racing as he felt her beauty draw him powerfully toward her. "I shouldn't allow her charm to carry me away like this," he reasoned hazily. "I don't know her true character yet." His thoughts about her were interrupted when she spoke.

"It looks like you got shot and Irwin got clubbed over the head because of presumptuous faith and the fact that certain precautions weren't taken."

Brian saw the mature young figure stiffen as the impact of the thought came to her. "Exactly!" Brian snapped back indignantly. "I'm afraid I'm in Dutch again with your father for I've had real convictions about these principles, and other principles, too. I had to give in for the sake of unity—if you can call that unity. If I were more dogmatic in trying to follow my convictions, I wouldn't be here. Then, too, probably not in the mission either, for causing more trouble over it."

"I see your point." June shook her head in dismay. "I'm sorry it turned out this way. There are quite a few folk in our mission who feel the way you do."

"I know," Brian said, his disturbed feelings evident in his voice. "I saw that last night."

"Saw what?"

"By the fact that Jim and Dick came in to help and they were armed to the teeth."

June's eyes narrowed as she asked, "You mean to tell me you guys didn't take guns?"

"We were told we couldn't. But . . ." Brian suddenly caught himself about to discuss what he had done to save Irwin's life but suddenly realized it would be best to keep quiet.

"But what?"

"Never mind. Enough said, I guess," Brian replied.

A bewildered look flickered in June's eyes as she looked up to see a couple of doctors coming in to check on their patient. They looked at his chart and then chatted amiably for a few minutes.

The next two days Brian continually improved, although he had a two-degree fever that gave the doctors concern. He thrilled at the opportunities to know June more intimately during the hours she cared for him. They were pleasant hours, even though pain often jabbed at him. She read the Scriptures to him and they felt a new closeness as they prayed together. He scarcely noticed that her praying seemed more mechanical than spontaneous.

The morning of the third day he woke as the sun came over the tree tops and blazed a dust-particle trail into the cream-colored room. June was standing beside the bed for she had just come on duty.

"Wow!" Brian beamed. "I see an indescribably beautiful creature. Where am I?"

"You're in a hospital bed and a human being is standing beside you." June's cheeks flushed as she lingeringly held his wrist to count his pulse. "When are you going to shave? You look like a bum."

"I'll shave as soon as you bring me hot water and when I finish telling you that it's a tremendous pleasure to have you for my private nurse."

June smiled affectionately. "I was glad they took up my offer when I volunteered. It's a pleasure to be able to nurse you back to health." Just then her signal on the buzzer in the hallway called her attention and she hurriedly slipped out through the open door.

When she came back in she cranked up the bed a little so Brian could shave. "That was Dad. He just got in from Rio and says he'll be over later this morning to see you."

Brian's face clouded as he wondered what Mr. Weatherton's mood would be. Would his relationship with the director cause a strain between himself and June? Would June help to soothe her father's roughness and quick judgment? Was he right in thinking that June might be used by the Lord to bring about a better relationship between her father and himself? For the time being her attractiveness was like a drug that deadened the realities which threatened.

Shortly after Brian had shaved and eaten breakfast, Mr. Weatherton came into the room. He was still wearing his suit coat. After kissing June mechanically on the cheek he extended his soft hand to Brian.

"How are you, Brian? I was very sorry to hear about your accident." He sat on the chair offered him by his daughter. "Tell me about your trip and what went on when you set up camp." June slipped around to the other side of the bed to put a thermometer under Brian's arm.

That's strange, he thought. *That is the first time I remember the director calling me by my first name, What's up?* He related the events which had occurred prior to the attack, and then continued his account. "I was talking on the radio when all of a sudden I looked out and there was a whole bunch of savages all painted up, yelling and heading our way. I heard Irwin holler for us to head for the river. He started in that direction but was knocked down by the lance of a savage. The Indian ran off. Then arrows began to fly when I went outside the hut and one hit me. Shortly the savages took off. Praise the Lord the other arrows didn't touch us," he concluded.

The friendly facade faded from the director's face and he began to look serious. "What do you suppose provoked their attack? Something must have been wrong, especially when we have the promises of God to protect and care for us."

"Who knows what provoked their attack?" Brian said with a shrug. "I suppose they don't want anyone to intrude on their territory. I wouldn't either if I lived like them."

"That's not the point," Weatherton replied, raising his voice like the wind in an increasing storm. "Jesus died on the cross for those Indians as well as for us. He is more concerned to see them reached with the message of salvation than we are. Therefore, He will prepare the way, so when things go wrong we may suspect there is sin and lack of unity."

Brian could see the battle in his eyes and was sure Irwin had written to him about their differences of opinion. His heart was racing as if preparing for battle also. Pain jabbed at him and he felt his face growing hot.

"I agree with you on most of your points. The only questions I have are: what do you call sin in this case and what's your basis of unity?" Apprehension etched lines on Brian's tanned forehead.

"Perhaps the best way to explain what I mean is to read part of Irwin's letter." He pulled it out of his inner pocket as his face grew iron-hard.

"He says,". . . as I said before, I don't know what happened after I was knocked out but I'm sure the Lord undertook and caused the savages to suddenly forsake their evil intentions. This bears out His promises to care for His own. If there had been unity, not even this would have happened. We reaped suddenly that which was sowed. Brian has continually opposed most of my directions. First he said I was wrong in not taking in five men; then, until I put my foot down, he was insistent that we take guns. Later he questioned my judgment about staying in this campsite. If he had been in unity with us, the Lord would have blessed and even restrained the savages from attacking us.' "

Brian swallowed hard. He hurt deep within, not because of the arrow wound, but because of the criticism of a friend who misjudged his motives. He longed to help Irwin, who seemed to be enslaved by Mr. Weatherton and to lack complete dedication to Jesus Christ and His principles as plainly seen in the Scriptures. "Oh, Irwin," he thought, fighting back the tears, "how can you do this to me? If you only knew how I saved your life! How I've prayed for you and yearned to have deep fellowship with you!" His thoughts were disturbed by the sharp voice of the director.

"What do you have to say concerning what Mr. Gates wrote?"

Brian was deeply disturbed. Waves of heat rolled over his skin. Should he boast of what he had done to save Irwin's life and thereby save his own reputation now? Would not God in some way vindicate the truth? What would June think of Irwin's accusations? He looked at her and saw that she appeared to be deeply perplexed. Brian spoke with effort. "Before you pass too harsh a judgment on me I suggest you check with Roy for all the facts. Irwin hasn't told you all that happened."

"He's told me enough," the older man snapped. "And the same trouble exists that I warned you about when you were here studying the language. I told you if you didn't prove yourself out in the jungle, you would be a man without a mission board. Right?"

June's mouth dropped as she lifted her hand to conceal her surprise. "Father, I don't think this is the place and time to be discussing such matters. Remember Brian is dangerously sick yet. He was close to death. His temperature has already gone up since you've been here. Couldn't you wait until he's better?" She was looking at the thermometer that she had forgotton and left under his arm.

"June, I didn't ask for your opinion," her father spoke sternly. The reproach in his voice made Brian wince. He got up on his elbow and his face burned with resentment.

"All right, Mr. Weatherton. Let me tell you what really happened. Just after Irwin . . ." The door had been opened and just then the doctor came in, his eyes blazing.

"What's going on in here?" he roared. "Brian, what are you doing up on your elbows? Look at your face. You're flushed with fever. I gave strict orders that you were to be quiet."

Then, looking hard at June, he continued angrily. "Miss Weatherton, why is it you are not carrying out my orders? You want this man to die on your hands? Who is this visitor? He has no right to be in here. How come there's no sign on the door to keep visitors out? What's Brian's temperature?"

June looked again at the thermometer as her cheeks flushed rosy red. "It's . . . it's a hundred and four degrees." Her mouth dropped with alarm.

"One hundred and four!" the doctor roared. "That's terribly serious. Get the alcohol. We've got to bathe him with it and get that temperature down."

Then, with both hands on his hips and staring intently, he turned and thundered, "Whoever you are, mister, please leave the room immediately."

The doctor whirled to face June, who had gone to the table on the far side of the room to get the alcohol. Brian saw the tears streaming down her face.

"Who is this man anyway and why is he coming in here and talking heatedly to Brian? Look what he's done." The doctor looked hard at June once again.

The director was already halfway across the room as June sobbed out, "He's . . . he's my father. I'm sorry. I tried to . . ." She couldn't talk further as she sobbed uncontrollably, putting her hands to her face.

"Father or not, I demand that no more visitors be allowed in here until I tell you. Understand?" The doctor shook his finger at her and she nodded in agreement.

The doctor continued more calmly. "Let's swab this man all over with that alcohol." Then, helping Brian to sit up, he began to tap him at various places on his chest and back. He also listened with his stethescope.

Brian sighed deeply and said exhaustedly, "What's up, Doc?"

The physician's face clouded as he continued to tap. "Your injured lung is beginning to fill up with fluid," he said gravely.

"What does that mean, Doc?" Brian questioned.

"Likely pneumonia," the doctor retorted. With that he began to write instructions on the chart. Then he asked June, whose sobbing had subsided, to step outside for a moment with him for consultation.

A few minutes later June was back. Closing the door, she rushed over to Brian and fell upon his neck and wept. "I'm sorry, darling," she sobbed.

"You couldn't help it, honey," Brian assured her, after swallowing hard before he could speak. The sudden unexpected endearing words that escaped from his own lips and from June's surprised him and at the same time shook his very being with emotion. *June really loves me,* he thought. *And it must be I'm in love with her. Should I tell her? Or should I wait to be sure of my own heart and emotions? Will this pass away?*

After a bit she wiped her tears from his face and hurriedly got the alcohol bottle so that she could swab him to bring down his temperature.

"I sure feel bushed," he said after she had finished and again stuck the thermometer under his arm.

"No wonder, going through an ordeal like that," she said sympathetically. "I have to give you another shot and then you must go to sleep."

Late in the afternoon Brian awoke when he heard a couple of doctors talking with June at the foot of the bed. He noticed that the door had been left open and on it was a sign, "No visitors, please." He heard them comment that his temperature was down to a hundred degrees. After the doctors had left, June asked. "Did you see the letters beside you?"

"No," he said as he started to turn to get them.

"Just a minute," June replied, walking over to get them. "I'll get them for you."

"How about you reading them to me, honey?" Brian smiled.

"Here's one from your mom," June said, tearing it open. She read the first paragraph. The second paragraph began, "Last Tuesday I was ironing in the afternoon. Somehow I felt a real burden in my heart to pray for you. It was a strange feeling that's hard to explain. I felt you were in trouble. I pulled out the iron plug and went into the front room and got on my knees to pray for you. It was over half an hour before the burden lifted. Did anything happen on that day? When your father came home for supper I told him about it. It was a late supper as he worked overtime. So at the supper table, just before dark, we prayed again for you."

June laid the letter on the bed and exclaimed, "That's the very moment, darling, when you were being attacked and Mike barely got in with the plane!"

Brian swallowed hard as tears welled up in his eyes. "Praise God for a mother that can hear the voice of the Lord and is quick to obey and pray. The prayers of my folks mean more to me and are more effective than the prayers of the whole church. Her prayers and Dad's move the hand of God."

June continued to read. "I haven't been feeling too well of late ...Continue to make a stand for the truth no matter what it costs ..."

She looked up from the letter and spoke softly. "Praise God for parents like that. I wish my dad's prayers were moving the hand of God as they used to. I . . . " Her voice broke.

Brian searched her brown eyes as her lips quivered. His heart ached for her. He knew this experience was a strain on her also. She read the other letters and when she had finished he asked, "What's new on the radio from the fellas in the Panube area?"

"They said they moved camp to somewhere upriver about an hour by boat. Nothing more has been seen of the savages," she replied as she went to open the curtains.

"Well, can you beat that!" Brian said, scratching his head as he pondered the change of location.

"Beat what?" the young lady asked with a question in her eyes.

"Oh, I guess I was just thinking out loud. Not too important," he explained.

"I bet I know what you were thinking."

"What?"

"About what Irwin mentioned in his letter," June continued, "the matter of thinking you were wrong when you said you thought it would be better to go upriver farther to make a new camp."

"Yeah, you guessed it," Brian said, looking puzzled.

Toward evening, just before June went off duty Brian was sleeping restlessly. His disturbing dreams of savages caused him to toss and turn upon his bed. Then he felt something very soft touching his lips. What was it? He opened his eyes just as June began to straighten up. She had tenderly kissed him. His thoughts whirled in confusion. The emotion thrilled him through and through, yet he wondered if it was premature. It was too late to do anything about it and he wondered if he should say anything. He didn't as he was not sure of his own heart's convictions.

"I'm going off duty, honey." She spoke softly. "See you tomorrow." She slipped through the open door and was gone.

A few minutes later another nurse came in and picked up his chart. "Well, Evelyn! What are you doing here? I thought you were out in one of the tribes."

She smiled wearily as she put a thermometer under his arm. "Hi, Brian. Sorry to see you here in this condition. How are you feeling now?"

Brian studied her as she waited for the thermometer to register. She was about as tall as June, but slightly heavier. Her attractive face and features reminded him a little of his mother. Virtue was written across her serene face.

"I feel pretty good right now except I'm starving on this liquid diet. I'm anxious to know how you happen to be here."

When she pulled out the thermometer she began to speak softly. "I came out of the tribe last week as I haven't been feeling well. I wanted to get some rest and tests and a check-up. Today the hospital staff called at the mission home and asked if there was anyone who could substitute tonight as the night nurse was sick. I told Mr. Weatherton I thought I could handle it for a few nights. I guess the nurse got the flu."

After jotting something on the chart she said, "I'll be back about midnight to give you another shot. If you need anything beforehand, give me a buzz." With that she smiled and went out.

The wind whistled through the screened window but Brian didn't think it would rain, for the dry season had begun and most of the threatening storms did not develop. However, the cool breeze stirred his yearning to sleep again. It had been a historic day in more ways than one, he thought. Would this day have a bearing on the events of the future? Soon his thoughts blurred and he drifted off to sleep.

He was awakened in the morning by a strange yet friendly feminine voice that spoke in Portuguese. Brian shook his foggy head and asked, "Where's June this morning?"

"She was changed to the ward on the lower floor. I was sent up to take this section. Whatever you need, señor, just give me a call."

"Oh, no!" Brian moaned inwardly. "That seems strange. What's behind this change?"

CHAPTER SIX

Five lonely days had passed since June was transferred, and Brian wondered why she hadn't been up to see him. There had been continual improvement in his health. Finally one evening, during visiting hours, there was a knock on the door. It was June. Immediately Brian tingled with excitement.

"What a sight for sore eyes!" he exclaimed, watching her lovely face as she slipped over to him. "Where in the world have you been?"

She leaned over and kissed him tenderly. "Good to see you, darling." She glowed as she straightened up. "I just got off duty so I hurried up to see how you were doing."

"How come you didn't come these past days? Was something wrong?" he asked searchingly.

"I wanted to come but couldn't make it," she replied as her face became troubled and she gazed at the floor.

"Why were you transferred?"

"I don't know."

"Why couldn't you at least get up to see me a few minutes?" he asked again soberly.

"Dad wanted me to come home immediately after duty as he said he needed my help to get out some correspondence," June said falteringly.

"Do you think that is really the reason, honey?" he asked, taking her hands.

June sat beside the bed and Brian could see that she was silently pondering his question. Then she spoke. "I guess not. Dad was pretty upset by the tongue-lashing from the doctor and what happened out in the Panube camp with you men. Things don't look too good for you. I'm sorry things went as they did. I . . ." Her voice broke as tears flooded her eyes. She laid her head on the edge of the bed over Brian's arm.

"I understand, darling," Brian swallowed hard several times to hold back his own emotion. "Let's pray for your father. Perhaps he's run down physically and it's affecting his spiritual life, too."

June looked up with wet eyes. "I've never seen Dad like this. Mom and I are both deeply concerned." She sighed deeply. "I don't know what to do."

"Pray that one of these days I'll have the opportunity to speak to him about the needs in his life," Brian said softly, his face troubled.

"Do you dare approach him about things in his life after what happened five days ago?" June asked with surprise in her eyes.

"Before God we are responsible for each other's spiritual and physical well-being. Therefore, if the Lord leads, I have no other choice. Let's pray together now."

They prayed. His heart went out to Mr. Weatherton. He felt that the director was not basically a hard man, but because he did not walk in close fellowship with the Lord, had become enslaved by his own emotions and reasoning.

"I must hurry," June said after they had prayed. Brian wanted her to stay longer but understood why she must leave.

Five more days passed in the hospital and June came once more during that time. The doctors finally gave him permission to leave and it was an exciting day.

At the mission base he often sat in the living room to study and read. This afforded him more opportunities to see June at breakfast time before she went on duty and at coffee time in the evening after she came home. Often as Mr. Weatherton passed through the living room he spoke kindly but hadn't paused to converse. Then one day the director asked, "I understand you can type well."

"Guess maybe I can hold my own when it comes to typing. Is there something I can do for you?" Brian asked eagerly.

"Yes, you can, if you will." The director responded matter-of-factly. "I have about a hundred letters I'd like to get out this week. They are all the same. I'd like them typed so as to make them more personal."

"Sure, I'll be glad to," Brian assured him. The elderly graying man thanked him and said he'd give him a copy in the morning. Brian appreciated the opportunity. Perhaps this little job would draw them closer together. Brian yearned for the time when they would have complete trust and confidence in each other and be able to pray together. Then, too, he reasoned, if relations between him and the director were less strained, perhaps he and June could have more time together. Was he right, he asked himself, in believing that her father, in a very diplomatic way, was trying to keep them from going together?

The next morning Brian felt bright and hopeful as the morning mist began to retreat before the rising tropical sun. It felt good to be able to take a deep breath without pain. Maybe this would be the day, he thought, when things would be improved by his doing Mr. Weatherton a favor. Somehow, Brian reasoned, this was like taking an aspirin to dull the pain. To clear up the difficulties it would be necessary to get to the source, the attitude and the heart of the man. He hoped that nevertheless this day would at least be a steppingstone in the right direction.

"Good morning, Mr. Weatherton." Brian beamed hopefully as he entered his office. "Do you have the letter ready for me to start copying?"

"Yes, just a minute," the director replied as he began to search the cluttered desk. He found the letter and handed it to Brian. "Here is the stationery, addresses and envelopes. You can use that desk and typewriter over by the wall if you like."

Brian began with the efficiency of a skilled typist. When he reached the second page, however, his typing slowed considerably. He stopped and studied the letter. He could feel the temperature of his blood rising as he wondered if Mr. Weatherton was really truthful about what he wrote. "Oh, well," Brian concluded as he began typing again, "I'd better keep quiet and keep peace in the family. I guess it's really none of my business." As he finished the first letter his countenance clouded and he felt as if he were carrying a heavy packsack on his back.

The second letter was more difficult to type when he came to the second page and copied the same message. His conscience was uneasy. He could hear the words of his mother: "Continue to make a stand for the truth no matter what it costs." *Maybe I don't understand all that's involved. Mr. Weatherton may be telling the truth,* Brian reasoned. Yet this didn't soothe his conscience. *If I approach him about this, it'll be the ax for me. It's not worth it.* He continued to type and his heart became heavier.

No point in kidding myself any longer, Brian decided as he flipped the paper into the typewriter to start the fourth letter. *There is something wrong and I must check with Mr. Weatherton.* A sudden chill went up his spine at the very thought of talking with him. It seemed as if a dark cloud suddenly loomed before him and threatened his future. "Continue to make a stand for the truth no matter what it costs." He heard the words again as if his mother were standing before him and looking passionately into his eyes.

"Mr. Weatherton," Brian began, turning around to face him. "Maybe you could clear up a question that's bothering me."

The director looked up, taking off his heavy-rimmed glasses. "Yes, what is it?"

Brian took a deep breath as he referred to the copy of the letter. "It says here that you need fifty thousand dollars for expansion of the Bible institute. If I remember correctly, a few months ago at devotions, you mentioned you were going to build another girls' and boys' dormitory but were going to keep it very simple. Therefore the two buildings, you said, wouldn't cost much more than seven or eight thousand dollars. How do you figure you need fifty thousand?"

Tension filled the air as Brian could see the director's face burn. "Are you questioning my integrity?" the elderly man snapped.

"I didn't ask concerning that," Brian began seriously. "I want to clear up my own thinking and conscience because I'm wondering why the two figures don't match. Perhaps you have something else in mind that I haven't heard."

"True, the cost will run, we figure now, up to ten thousand dollars," the flushed face man began. "I mentioned fifty thousand dollars in case it runs a bit more unexpectedly, and what is left over we need in the general fund for other matters." He spoke defensively.

"Isn't that stretching it a little too much?" Brian queried.

"Well, I don't know," the director retorted with emphasis. When people give, they give as unto the Lord. When we use the funds for the Lord's work in some other way, what's the difference?"

"If I were the one giving, I'd give for one thing but not necessarily for another. I'd want to know exactly what my money was being used for as I'd have to give an account to God." Brian spoke with conviction in his voice, yet with caution.

"Are you implying I'm mishandling the funds?" the director asked with consternation in his tired eyes.

"No, no, Mr. Weatherton. I have no reason to believe so."

"Frankly, it is none of your business how the funds are handled. It's up to our field council and myself." There was a cold pause.

The words cut deeply into Brian and he prayed silently that God would give him wisdom to answer. He felt assured that God would help as he spoke. "Mr. Weatherton, I want to speak with all the kindness I know. I believe this is my business and the business of every missionary in our mission. We make up the mission. We represent our mission wherever we go. If people question our mission as to the way things are done, we missionaries are the losers and God's work suffers."

"You go to extremes in your thinking, Mr. Allmand. As I said before, you have the responsibility to be submissive to my authority because God put me here as director of this mission."

"I wish to be in submission to you, Mr. Weatherton," Brian began meekly. "I recognize that those in authority are in continual spiritual battle and that's why I've prayed much for you in recent days. I think you've been overworked these past months. I'm wondering if you have become so loaded down with the work and responsibilities that little by little you have been spending less time in fellowship with the Lord. When anyone fails to keep a close contact with the Lord in prayer, the works of the flesh are bound to take over. These thoughts have run through my mind lately as I've prayed for you."

"That's not the problem," Mr. Weatherton inserted.

"Perhaps not," Brian continued, hoping he was hitting the nail on the head. "I have noticed that you've become increasingly burdened. I trust you won't consider me intruding, but hasn't the pressure of the work stolen from you some of the peace and joy you had experienced for many years before?"

The director dropped his gaze and lowered his head. There was a long silence. Brian pulled out his handkerchief to wipe his brow. He felt that the Lord was very near and was speaking to the director's heart.

Finally the graying man looked up. His face had lost its cold look and had become troubled. "I guess you're right, Mr. Allmand. I hadn't realized it before. I've been working long hours and haven't been getting the proper rest. And as you say, I haven't been spending the proper time in the Word and prayer. Why didn't someone point this out to me before?"

Brian thought for a moment. "Let's face it, Mr. Weatherton, would you have taken such a rebuke before?"

"Probably not in this condition," he said, resting his chin in his cupped hands and staring at the cluttered desk.

"That's why no one approached you about it. I didn't want to myself for fear of an unfavorable reaction. But I have to live with my conscience twenty-four hours a day if I disobey the leading of the Lord." Brian realized that his body was still tense and he shifted in his chair to relax.

Mr. Weatherton looked up. The fire had gone out of his eyes. "Continue to pray for me. Let's make a change in that letter. Toss out the ones you've typed."

Brian felt as if a tremendous load had fallen from his back as he excused himself for a few minutes while the director changed the letter. Brian's thoughts were interrupted when he was part of the way across the patio.

"Hi, handsome." June beamed. "What happened to you? You look like you've been dragged through a keyhole."

Brian looked up. "Hi, honey, good to see you. How come you're not working today?"

"I got a day off. I'm on my way over to the kitchen for a snack. How about joining me?"

"Sounds good. I'll be right over in a jiff." He brightened as they went their ways. A few moments later the two sat at one of the dining-room tables enjoying each other's company.

"You didn't tell me why you looked so beat," June prodded with concern creasing her soft face. "Are you having more pain?"

Brian looked into her troubled eyes. Her silken hair flowed gently to her shoulders. Her vitality and love of life could be seen in every action.

"No, I'm feeling pretty good." He spoke softly.

She took another sip of coffee. "Don't tell me you and Dad had another powwow!"

"Sorry, we did. But I think things are going to turn out better."

"Dad's been real busy these past weeks and it's been wearing him down." She spoke sympathetically.

Brian gulped the last of his coffee and added. "Continue to pray for me, chick. I'm still a green missionary on probation. Oh, by the way, if you're free tonight, let's play a game of Scrabble and then go uptown for a treat." He rose to return to the office.

"Anything, as long as we can be together," June returned with a sparkle in her eyes.

"Another thing I was going to ask you and I keep forgetting. Whatever happened to that Saturday-night Bible study I used to have?"

"I heard it was turned over to another mission."

Brian raised his eyebrows. "Can you beat that!" There was disgust in his voice. Then he smiled and squeezed her hand. "See you tonight." There were many problems that still troubled him, but he reasoned that this was not the time to mention them. Sooner or later, however, he knew the subject would have to be discussed.

When the young missionary went back into the office the atmosphere was clean and fresh as it is after a tropical storm. The tense expectancy of something ominous about to happen was gone and there was the stillness like that which follows refreshing showers. Mr. Weatherton looked up and smiled as he gave Brian the revised copy of the letter. He read it and prepared to type several copies before the dinner bell rang.

The day seemed to go much faster than usual. No doubt this was because much of the strain between the senior and junior missionaries had been removed. Later as June and Brian were playing Scrabble at the coffee table in the corner of the living room, they looked up when the squeaky screen door opened.

"Hi, you all," Evelyn greeted, her crisp nurse's uniform rustling. "Who's getting the shellacking?"

"June spoke up. "This brain always beats me."

"Come on now." Brian spoke with a smile as Evelyn drew near. "None of this diplomatic stuff. Tell her the truth, how you give me a fit every once in awhile."

"Don't rush off," June said as Evelyn prepared to leave.

"I have to be on duty in a few minutes so I'll see you all later." Brian watched her as she went with a slight droop in her shoulders.

"She doesn't look at all well. Her face seems more troubled than when I first saw her right after she came up from the tribe." He spoke with concern in his voice.

"I think she'll be off substituting this week so I hope she gets some rest and some tests to see what her trouble is. The other day I noticed how nervous she was when she was holding a cup of coffee." June went back to figuring out her next play.

"Too bad," Brian said. "She's so young and already so beat."

Before long Mike came bouncing in. "Hi, you lovers. I see you're sharpening up your wits again at that game."

"Hi," Brian greeted, looking up at the pilot. "We're about to start another game so why not join us?"

"I'd like to get a crack at you but I gotta go in and see Mr. Weatherton. Conference is coming up in about a month and I want to see what he has in mind about who is coming out from the Panube camp—whether all the men will come or just Irwin. I've got a lot of flights to make to bring folk in so I was wondering if I should keep the pontoons on the plane. Of course I want to keep them on as long as possible in case the fellas need an emergency flight. See you later." Off across the living room he went to knock on the office door.

While June studied the Scrabble board, Brian studied the lovely creature before him. She was so full of life and easy to talk with. A few slight characteristics of her father could be noticed in her, however. Could her persuasiveness eventually turn into a domineering spirit? Brian erased such a thought from his mind. Nevertheless, he couldn't escape the nagging question: would her father approve of their friendship or try to separate them?

CHAPTER SEVEN

Brian was leaving the dining room when Evelyn came up to him. There were many missionaries milling about for it was only a few days before the conference.

"Hi, Brian," Evelyn greeted nervously. "I'd like to have a talk with you whenever you're free."

He looked down into her troubled eyes. Although, like Brian, she was in the mid-twenties, she looked tired and older. Her sparkle had gone and her attractive-featured face showed the strain of a heavy inward burden. She was neatly groomed, although the gloss had left her light brown hair.

"Sure, Eve," he replied slowly. "Let me see. How about shortly after dinner? We can meet in the living room. No doubt almost everyone will be taking a siesta and I'm sure we won't be disturbed."

"That'll be fine, Brian. I'm sure you can help me. See you later."

Before going to the office to type for Mr. Weatherton, he lingered longer in his room, praying and asking God to give him wisdom and discernment in helping Evelyn. His heart felt burdened; to him it seemed that her trouble was not basically physical but spiritual. Throughout the morning he couldn't get her out of his thoughts. She was in trouble and must be helped.

The young missionary was relieved when he saw the others making their way to their rooms after dinner, for he wondered what they might say if they saw him and Miss White talking together a long time.

"What can I do for you, Eve?" he asked with concern and sympathy in his eyes, as they sat down facing each other.

There was a moment of silence. She was nervously twisting her handkerchief in her lap. Her yellow-flowered sleeveless dress stood out like a bright candle in the dark. Taking a deep breath, she began. "I hate to bring my problems to you as I understand you have plenty of your own, but I'm sure you can help me." She looked up as she shifted her weight on the edge of the wicker chair.

"As you know, I came out from the tribe about the same time you did. I wasn't real sick, yet I knew I wasn't well either. The doctor couldn't find anything wrong with me so recommended I get some rest. He wanted me to take tranquillizers every day for two weeks. I didn't take any because I didn't want to start trusting in them in times of stress. Perhaps you've noticed I'm nervous. I can hardly sleep and often I have terrible nightmares. I can't figure it out for I've never had trouble sleeping before and my days are no more strenuous than those of the other missionaries."

Brian rested his arm on the armchair and studied the nearly broken young woman before him.

"I began to wonder if there might be something wrong spiritually that I was not aware of. I went to Mr. Weatherton for help. He read some Scripture passages to me and prayed for me and suggested I get plenty of rest. Then I talked with Mr. Gates. He felt I wasn't able to take the tropics and suggested I go back to the States."

"Brian," she looked pleadingly into his eyes, "I don't want to go back to the States. I've given my life to the Lord to reach these Indians for Christ and I can't stand the thought of giving it up." She raised her handkerchief to stop the tears that started coursing down her hollow cheeks.

"Let's pray, Eve, before we go any further, and ask the Lord to give wisdom and help." As he prayed he felt the very presence of the Lord with them.

"A thought came to me when I was praying," he said, leaning forward. "What were you doing the day before you noticed this nervous sensation or the first night you could hardly sleep?"

Evelyn was deep in thought for a few moments. "Let's see. First I think we had literacy classes and after that we had medical call. These two things generally take up most of the morning. In the afternoon we usually spend some time with our informant. He is helping us to translate Mark. Come to think of it, that afternoon the witch doctor came and pestered us for a machete. I told him I wouldn't give him one but that I would take something in trade for it. I figured I could get a souvenir. I have several bows and arrows so I asked him to trade his little bark bag similar to those which most of these Indians carry at their sides, with the straps slung over their shoulders. He got mad and stomped off."

Brian's eyes widened with interest. "What do they carry those little bags around for?"

"We're not sure, but we noticed that before they go hunting they reach into their bags, pull out the stones, rub them on their bodies, and then kiss them. One time when a bad storm came, several took their little stones out of the bags and held them to the wind and chanted."

"Sounds like the stones might be their gods," Brian said gravely as a chill went up his back.

"We've wondered about that, too," Evelyn said, sitting back farther in her chair.

"Then what?"

"The witch doctor had argued with me for over half an hour so my informant agreed to stay longer as I wanted to finish checking out the chapter we were on. Later the creepy-looking witch doctor came back with the little bag with the stone in it and said he'd trade it for the machete. I noticed the informant looked real surprised. He got up and left right away. I couldn't figure out why he acted so strange."

Brian drew in his lips and tightened his wide jaw as he nodded to Miss White that he was following every step of her conversation.

She went on. "Later that evening the chief came over, looking very troubled. He saw the little bag on my table and pointed to it and said I should throw it away as it would cause me harm. I just laughed and told him not to worry for a little stone and bag couldn't do anything. I . . ."

"Wait a minute!" Brian interrupted. "Was that the night you stayed awake most of the night for the first time?"

"I think it was," Eve replied.

"What were you thinking about during the night and did you have any dreams?" Seriousness deepened the lines around his tightened mouth.

"Come to think of it, that night I had the first nightmare I've had since I was a child. I could see little stones hurtling toward me from space. Then bigger ones. They all missed. Then one great big one came right for me and I awoke screaming, scaring Ida, my partner, nearly out of her wits. I've had several nightmares just like that. It's about driving me bugs. I . . ."

He could see she was getting tense as she began to clench her fists. "I think we've hit the core of your problem, Eve."

"What do you mean?" she asked with a shaky voice.

"That stone that the chief warned you about did and is doing just exactly what the chief said—causing trouble."

Evelyn's eyes widened and she stared glassily at the floor for a moment. "Do you really think a stone could cause that?"

"Not the stone but their god or, better understood, the very demon or demons they worship have molested and harassed you. Just recently I was reading a book about demon experiences and there was one similar to what you described."

"What happened in the case you read about?" she asked with a puzzled look in her eyes.

"She was told to get rid of the fetish and after she did so, her trouble cleared up. By the way, do you still have that stone?"

"Yes, it's over in my room." she spoke with a tight voice.

"Go get it," Brian said emphatically, "and let's take a walk down to the river and throw it in."

At the muddy river bank he took the little bag with the stone in it and heaved it as far as he could. "Away with you, demons, in the Name of Jesus Christ," he said vehemently. Then, turning to Evelyn, he said, "I think you've learned your lesson. Let's pray."

When Evelyn prayed she confessed to the Lord her wrong in taking the fetish and asked for a renewing of His love within, a new hunger for the Word of God and for fellowship with Him and for discernment so that she would not be ensnared again.

After Brian had prayed she looked up. "I feel like I'm walking on air. That was it! When you threw that bag into the river it felt like my heavy load went with it. The Lord sure gave you wisdom. Thank you so much for your time and help."

"I suggest," Brian began, as they both started walking toward the mission station, "that for your own good we get together a couple of evenings for a little Bible study on the authority of the believer. The devil will come back to give you a bad time, but we'll find in the Word how to take care of him. How about a few minutes of study tonight?"

"That sounds fine, but . . ."

"But what?" Brian asked, taking her arm as they crossed a narrow plank bridge over a small stream.

"But what will June say if she sees us together?"

"Don't worry. I'll talk to her about it and maybe she'll want to join in the study," he responded reassuringly.

June had to go on night duty. Several of the missionaries sat in the living room talking so Brian and Evelyn seated themselves at a table in the dining room, where the conversation of the others was merely a jumbled hum. Evelyn brought her aladdin lamp as she said she didn't like the hissing of a pressure lamp. "In the jungle I studied with the quiet aladdin lamp so I could hear if anything was going on outside," she explained.

Already Brian could see a new sparkle and liveliness in her eyes. Some of the lines of weariness were gone from her face and her youthful vitality had returned. With eagerness she listened as Brian showed her Scripture passages in which the word "power" meant "authority," and he pointed out to her that believers possess that authority to command the powers of darkness to flee. Their study was not completed that first evening, since there were still several other Scripture passages to be considered.

Later in the week, as the dawn painted an orange tinge on the jungle surrounding the mission station on the edge of town, Brian started down to the river to have his devotions. A little way from the house he met June as she was coming home from night duty at the hospital.

"Hi, honey," Brian said with an affectionate smile. "How you doing? You look tired."

"Hi, Brian," she responded coolly. "I had a rough night."

After a bit more conversation about what had occurred during the night, June asked, "Say, what happened to Evelyn? She suddenly seems so happy and well. I heard she came to you and since that time has been riding on a cloud. I suppose during your high school and college days many girls were elated like her when they were around you." There wasn't the warmth in her smile that Brian had seen so often before.

Brian laughed. "Now just a minute, honey. Nothing to be jealous about. Let me tell you about the tremendous victory in her life." As he began to tell her about Evelyn he reached over to take June's hand. She raised her hand at the same time as if to brush an imaginary hair from her face. Brian felt stabbed to the heart for he could see she was jealous and was visibly cool toward him. The hurt began to rise and it seemed to stick in his throat. While he was telling about Evelyn he didn't notice the huge ball of orange and red sun appear over the misty horizon.

June looked at her watch. "I must hurry home."

"Wait a minute, darling," Brian pleaded. "Don't be that way. I assure you of my love. When can we meet again?"

"I'll see how it goes," she replied as she left.

He stood awhile and watched her go. Dejectedly he sauntered down to the river with his Bible in his hand and then sat on a log overlooking the water below. He had no desire to pray or read. Hurt pierced him deeply. "Oh, Lord," he groaned, "why do these misunderstandings get in and cause heartache? There are the misunderstandings with Mr. Weatherton and Irwin. And now with June. I know there is a purpose because You allowed these things to touch me. Yet they hurt. Lord, I pray, work these problems out for Your honor and glory and for the furtherance of the Gospel."

During that first hour after sunrise the young missionary did not pray about the other matters he had jotted down on a list in his Bible, for his heart was too heavy. He tried to convince himself that this problem would pass and that things would again be well with the one he loved. Yet he didn't regret at all the time he had spent with Evelyn, for had he not helped her, she would have been another missionary going home in defeat.

The conference started that day and Brian enjoyed talking with the various missionaries and hearing about their work in other areas. Irwin had come out but the other men had preferred to stay in to build a couple of log cabins and get well entrenched. Already, three days before the conference, the field council had been meeting, as was customary. Brian noticed more formality in their greetings as he met and talked briefly with various members of the council. All, that is, except Mike. Mike was always very cordial and understanding and Brian was sure the pilot would stand up for him in their discussions. No doubt they talked about his convictions and how he clashed with Mr. Weatherton and Irwin. Perhaps, he reasoned, the director and his assistant were cool toward him because of their embarrassment resulting from their inability to discern Evelyn's problem and help her in her time of need.

June was at the afternoon meeting and Brian was thrilled to see that she was still willing to sit beside him. He wondered when they could be alone to talk things over, but since she was on night duty and had to sleep during the day, it wouldn't be possible, especially during the conference.

The speaker, who had come from the States for the conference, gave soul-stirring, heart-searching messages and Brian took notes. On the third day of the conference the field council asked Brian to come in for a talk. They talked to various missionaries in the early part of the afternoon when no meeting was scheduled.

They greeted Brian politely when he walked into the director's office.

Mr. Weatherton glanced up and invited him to take a seat. Taking off his glasses, which dangled from his hand, he began to speak. "Mr. Allmand, I have been discussing with the field council some of the early difficulties you had in getting adjusted to missionary work. I also told them about some of the differences of opinion you have had concerning the contact work. We just want to encourage you to realize that Mr. Gates is your senior missionary and the leader of this contact work and that when discussions come up and there are differences of opinion, he is to have the final decision. That will eliminate further friction and disunity." His severe glance bore into Brian. "There is one other matter, maybe two, that should be brought up at this time."

Brian breathed deeply as he looked over to Mike, wondering if he was agreeing with all that was being said. His kind face was troubled.

"It seems like, uh," Mr. Weatherton continued slowly, searching for proper words, "that, uh, well, I wonder if maybe you, uh, perhaps have a tendency to, shall we say, to go on a tangent on some thoughts."

A puzzled look clouded Brian's face. "I don't understand what you're getting at, Mr. Weatherton. Are you still referring to my convictions about having more men on the contact work, and carrying guns?"

"No, I was referring to, uh, or perhaps I should say that there seems to be a possibility that, uh, well, you may be going overboard in seeing the devil in every circumstance."

"It still isn't clear to me what you are referring to," Brian repeated, disgust evident in his voice, "unless you are referring to the difficulty that Evelyn White had recently. Is that what you mean?"

"Right. I know of a case where a missionary thought the devil was controlling a certain situation. They soon began to believe that when anything went wrong the devil was in the middle of it."

"Are you implying that is what I'm doing?" Brian asked with indignation.

"Not necessarily," the director said slowly. "But it sure is a beginning, as I can see. I just want to warn you to be on guard."

"Frankly I don't see where I've even begun to go on a tangent," Brian began with conviction in his voice. "Let's face the facts. Both

75

you and Mr. Gates tried to help her when she came to you. She received no help whatsoever. In fact she was more discouraged when Mr. Gates suggested that she go back to the States. She came to me and I knew I was helpless so I prayed the Lord would give me discernment and wisdom. I believe He did. The fact that she is free from depression and from having terrible nightmares and that she is back to robust health is proof enough that the powers of darkness had been afflicting her. It is proof enough that prayer and reading the Word were not sufficient. Action had to be taken besides." Brian could see consternation in the eyes of Irwin and the director, for their frustration and lack of power were evident to the rest of the council.

Brian was deeply disturbed for he had hoped that since his talk with Mr. Weatherton in the office, when he had suggested that perhaps the older man was overloading his schedule and not spending proper time in fellowship with the Lord, the director had changed his attitude and had replaced his harshness with a spirit of Christian love. Apparently, however, there had been no change. Nevertheless there was hope, for when Brian zeroed in with the truth there could be no denying it. The director had been forced, on that previous occasion, to acknowledge that what Brian had said was true.

"There is another matter I want to bring up, Mr. Allmand." Once again the director fidgeted with his glasses. "We have to be extremely careful in this Latin American culture. They don't think like we do. Things that are proper in our culture are not practiced down here. What I'm referring to is, uh, well, what I mean is, the people we are seen with."

"Are you referring to my going with your daughter?" Brian asked, looking steadily toward Mr. Weatherton, who hadn't raised his eyes for sometime.

"Well, I don't like to say anything, because she is my daughter, but it is, uh, well, a principle, no matter who the man is and who the lady is."

"I have been very careful not to do anything in conflict with the Brazilian culture, as we were taught in language school. I believe that if you ask anyone about it, he will back me up."

Mr. Weatherton leaned back in his swivel chair with an air of finality. "Well, to prevent any possible talk I request that you two stop going together." With that Mr. Weatherton rose. "I believe that will be all, Mr. Allmand. Thank you for your co-operation, and we trust things will go better in the days ahead."

Brian felt as if a thunderbolt had hit him. He was so dazed he couldn't remember if he had said anything when he walked out. Hatred welled up within him with red-hot fierceness. He knew it was wrong but he let it smolder within. He walked to his room and, sitting on the edge of his bed, he slammed his fist into the palm of the other hand and exclaimed, "What a dirty deal! You don't have a chance in this mission!"

CHAPTER EIGHT

It's wonderful to be on the way back, Brian thought as he looked out of the airplane window to the green jungle far below. *For awhile it didn't look like I'd make it.* He glanced up at Irwin, who was sitting next to the pilot. A smile of pity crossed Brian's face. *Here is a man in a difficult situation,* he thought. *Basically he's a man like most of us missionaries. He hungers for fellowship, yet often he is denied it because he feels he has to carry out the archaic ideas of the director. He wants to be buddy-buddy with all of us but has to keep everyone at arm's length in order to maintain strict authority. He was surely shaken when Dick and Jim came in with guns, but down deep I think he appreciated the added protection and I don't believe it violated his faith.*

The hum of the motor and the thinner air made him drowsy. Thoughts of the past crowded out his prayer that Irwin would soon be a warm friend, with whom he could enjoy close fellowship. As his thoughts reached into the past days, the joy of flying back to the contact area yielded to a heavy heart and a troublesome conscience. He knew it was wrong to keep bitterness and hatred in his heart toward Mr. Weatherton. Two days before he had left the base he had asked the director if he could have a talk with him. He had wanted to apologize for his feelings at least, even though he believed that the elderly man was wrong in some of his ideas and actions. The director had said that he was busy at the time and would be occupied for the next two days.

Then Brian had tried to see June long enough to discuss the matter but she was never available. What had Mr. Weatherton told his daughter? Was she now ashamed of him besides being jealous because he had spent time helping Evelyn? Was her love for him so shallow that it could be disturbed and tossed about by her father's stormy outbursts?

78

Pressure change caused Brian's ear to "pop." He looked out again and could see that Mike had lowered their altitude so that they could fly under a cloud formation. Huge fluffy white clouds sped past his window and the dazzling brightness made him close his eyes.

"There's the smoke up ahead." Mike spoke loudly, above the noise of the motor. Then he lifted his microphone once again to report to the base as well as the camp that he was in sight of the smoke signal.

While the plane was taxiing up to the sandbar Brian could see Dick, Jim and Roy waving.

"Man, is it ever good to see you, Brian!" Roy exclaimed as soon as the door was opened. Both Jim and Dick gave him an *abrazo* (a South American hug that has deeper significance than a hand-shake).

"It's tremendous to be back with you men. We've got lots to talk about but first I'll hand you the cargo from inside." Brian took off his work shirt and climbed back into the plane to hand down the various-shaped boxes and bags. Irwin was up the sand-bar a few feet talking with Mike. When everything was unloaded Mike said he would have to go back immediately as he had to re-move the pontoons and make another flight that afternoon to take another couple out to their station.

Shortly Brian climbed the embankment with a sack of sugar over his shoulder. The new camp looked almost like a park as about five acres of jungle underbrush had been cleared away. Before him stood a two-floor log cabin with aluminum roofing. Mud had been packed between the logs. He gave a long whistle and said, "The only thing lacking here is to see you guys dressed up like Pilgrims and carrying your powder bags and muskets."

The afternoon went by swiftly with the unpacking of supplies, the exchanging of hunting and fishing experiences and the work which Brian had heard the other missionaries describe during the conference. The sky had deepened its purple glow in the west and the flames were already dancing as the five men crouched around the fire for an evening of fellowship and discussion of future plans.

"What do you say we sing awhile, men?" Dick asked enthu-siastically. "Now we can expand our trio to a choir."

"Maybe we can call ourselves the T-Shirt Brigade," Jim added with a chuckle.

Everyone sang heartily for about an hour and Brian felt good inside to see the initiative and enthusiasm of both Dick and Jim. Even Roy seemed to be more outgoing than before. *This is more like I envisioned missionary work to be,* Brian thought. *This fellowship and kindredship is inspiring.*

After a time of prayer Irwin spoke. "Now that we have five men in camp, we can make plans for the days ahead. While in town I went over to the National Geodetic Survey to see if they had any aerial maps of our area. After studying the area I think I pretty well figured out where our camp is. If my guess is right, there is a stream that empties about a mile upriver. Then up this stream about fifteen miles I spotted what looks like an Indian village. That would be roughly straight southwest from here."

"Wow, can you beat that!" Brian exclaimed. "What else did you find?"

"The Army sergeant," Irwin spoke seriously and authoritatively, "said, as he looked into the stereoscope, that apparently a huge section of the jungle south of us is swampy so it doesn't seem as if we can do any trail-making off that way. On the west side of this small river I was telling about, there seems to be high ground."

Jim got up and pushed three dry logs toward the center of the fire. Brian watched the sparks fly upward as the wood crackled vigorously and the fire blazed with new brilliance. The surrounding trees stood like sentinels guarding the beachhead which the band of missionaries had made on the hostile territory.

"My idea is to go to the west side of the stream and cut a trail southwest parallel with the stream." Irwin continued with an air of certainty. "If we follow the little river, we'll end up doing three times more trail-making, since it winds back and forth."

"Sounds good," Brian began with enthusiasm in his voice. "I'd like to make one suggestion and see what all of you men think. Most likely these savages hunt along this stream. I suggest we make the trail only two thirds of the way to their village and then leave gifts every mile. Instead of entering the jungle every day at a risk, we could go up just to the mouth of the stream in our boat and check the gifts that were left in the small clearing we could make."

Brian saw Irwin take a deep breath and sigh disgustedly. Even the other men noticed it as they looked up from staring at the fire. He continued. "One other suggestion. While we all work together on this trail I think Jim and Dick should take their guns along.

Then about every quarter mile we should make a perpendicular trail to the stream. This would serve as a means of escape should we meet a group of hunters head-on, or if they should ambush us from behind. Naturally we hope they'll be friendly but if they aren't, we should be prepared." Brian saw Jim and Dick nodding approval. "Then I propose . . ."

"Just a minute," Irwin cut in sharply. "I see you are still walking by sight and not by faith. That's just the reason we didn't have the full protection of the Lord when the savages attacked. Your philosophy is anti-Scriptural. God in His mercy undertook for us miraculously, but if we all had been united in believing God for the seeming impossible, I'm sure we would have made a friendly contact a couple of months ago. I hope we don't make the same mistake and end worse the next time."

"Wait a minute, Irwin." Roy spoke with disgust in his voice. Brian looked up in surprise as Roy had usually been silent in past debates. "This time we'd better listen to what Brian has to say! The time has come when you should know the full truth. You'd be six feet under if it weren't for what Brian did."

"How's that?" Irwin shot back with a puzzled expression.

"When you got knocked out, a savage crept up and drew his bow back to finish you off. Brian saw him and dived on top of you to protect you. That's how he got the arrow in his side that nearly cost him his life. I know for a fact that he has had a real love and concern for your spiritual welfare. That's why he risked his own life for yours."

Irwin's jaw dropped and his dark eyes widened. Even Dick and Jim hadn't heard this part of the story and likewise sat with their mouths open.

Roy went on, waving his arm and gesturing as if he were preaching to a huge crowd. "Before we came up here Brian had real conviction in his heart to carry his revolver hidden under his belt. He obeyed your order not to take a rifle. When he was lying on top of you with an arrow in his side, dozens of savages closed in to kill us all off. Arrows were flying at us. I dived for Brian and grabbed his revolver for I knew he had it. I shot up in the air several times and the savages tore off like scared rabbits. Your principles would have carried us all to our graves. If Brian's principle of caution combined with the realization that we must still trust in the Lord to guide and direct, had been carried out to the fullest, we would have taken five men armed with guns in the first place, and I don't think you or Brian would have been injured."

There was silence for a few moments. Everyone was too stunned to speak. Then Roy added with conviction, "Brian asked me not to tell anyone about his heroism. Perhaps I owe him an apology now for saying these things, but if I didn't say anything, we would all be exposed carelessly to these savages. And no one knows what the end results might be. Judging from what I've read about other missionaries who have done this kind of dangerous work, we should go slow and take all the precautions. They have proved that this principle works, for in one to three years the Indians were convinced that the missionaries meant no harm and a friendly contact was established."

Brian stood up to stretch. Everyone was silent, looking blankly into the fire. Then Irwin got up slowly. "I . . ." He choked with emotion and then walked over to Brian. Flinging his arms around him, he wept on his shoulders. Tears flooded Brian's eyes as he embraced his brother in Christ. "I'm . . . sorry . . . Brian . . . please . . . forgive me."

Brian embraced him all the tighter to express his forgiveness and love. Far beyond civilization, where the white man had never trod and where dangers abounded, the five missionaries held an unforgettable prayer and praise meeting. The jungle was silent as their shadows moved among the trees. It seemed that even the animals and roosting birds and frogs were quiet as if in worship of their Creator.

Later as they sat around the fire, Irwin confessed his opposition to Brian's spiritual principles. Basically he believed as Brian did, but he felt that he had to defend Mr. Weatherton's convictions. He admitted that his heart was deeply troubled and that he was hypocritical in defending a principle that was not his own conviction. He knew that his own spiritual life was barren and meaningless and that no amount of talk could bolster his own faith.

Tears of joy coursed down Brian's cheeks as he felt new love surging through his veins. For the first time the experience of true unity in the Lord warmed his heart. Now there would be greater joy in spiritual conquest, greater determination to reach the tribe for Christ, in spite of insects, and heat. "One other thing," Brian added as they prayed about various matters. "I guess you know that my relations with Mr. Weatherton have been strained and that I was nearly dismissed from the mission." He looked up and saw surprise registered on the faces of Dick and Jim. "Pray with me that things will clear up. I've had bitterness in my heart toward him because of some things I felt were unjust. For two days before coming back, I tried to see him to square things away, but he didn't have time. Pray that it may work out for me to talk with him sometime to make things right."

Late in the night everyone went inside the log cabin to go to bed, but Irwin said he was going to stay up a bit longer as he wanted to write a letter. Brian was sure he was going to write to the director, and he was also certain that the content of this letter would be entirely different from that in the letter he had written after the attack of the savages. Brian's heart was light and happy and sleep came almost immediately.

Irwin was the first one up in the morning and whistled softly while preparing breakfast. Cheerfully he called to the others to get up, for the night before they had agreed to get an early start at trail-making. Everyone pitched in to help with the preparations, which included making a lunch to take with them so that no time would be wasted in cooking on the trail.

For the next three days progress was slow. The jungle underbrush was thick and snagged with vines. The men guessed that they had gone about four miles during those three days. Then too they took time out to make the short trails every quarter mile toward the creek. This afforded them the opportunity to get a cool, fresh drink now and then. Every half mile gifts of beads and knives were hung and at the small clearing at the mouth of the river an ax was hung also.

There had been tense moments when they cut silently through the jungle without talking. Suddenly a quail from a near-by nest on the jungle floor had startled them as it roared off through the foliage. Quite often a hornet's nest had been hit by a machete and everyone had scampered down the trail. Then a detour had been necessary, giving a wide berth to the aggravated hornets. It had been agreed earlier that for the present there would be no hunting so as not to frighten the Indians should they be hunting in the jungle within hearing distance. The missionaries did not want the savages to know that the trail was being cut. Later, when the Indians discovered the gifts, they would follow them out to the clearing, where it would be much safer to meet them. All seemed to be going according to plan until the fourth day.

The men had already been walking more than an hour and hadn't yet come to where they had left off cutting trail the day before. Dick was in the lead with his shotgun and Jim, also carrying his rifle, was the last. Brian was second in line as they passed one of the trails that went down to the stream. Suddenly every man froze simultaneously. They all heard it. Right behind them a few hundred feet drums began beating.

"They've seen us!" Brian exclaimed.

"Listen!" Irwin said, breathing heavily. "Up ahead some more are signaling back. There now," he pointed to the right, "more are signaling."

The men waited a few moments in silence as the savages continued to beat their drums.

"They're closing in. Those drums sure sound agitated," Brian whispered.

"What do you think, fellas?" Irwin asked, his eyes searching the heavy undergrowth. Suddenly the drums stopped. Brian reasoned that the savages were having a war council.

"We'd better take off on the double down the trail toward the river and get over into the swamp where they won't likely follow us," Brian said, putting his hands over his revolver.

Just then an arrow whizzed overhead. "There's our answer!" Roy exclaimed.

The five men raced down the twisting trail toward the stream. In five minutes they reached the bank. Brian gasped for breath as he looked back over his shoulders to see how close the savages were. Fastening the strap over his revolver so it wouldn't fall out of the holster, he dived into the cool water just behind the other men. After swimming about a hundred and fifty feet he came to the slight embankment on the far side. It tapered off to the muddy swamp farther in. Just past the embankment the men stopped and waited for Brian. They were standing in water up to their hips, panting heavily. Brian pulled his shirt loose as it was clinging soggily to his body. "If only Mama could see me now!" he exclaimed. Everyone roared and it helped to break the tension.

"Got your compass yet, Irwin?" Dick asked, searching the jungle with his eyes.

"Yeah, I still got it," Irwin replied, digging it out of his pocket. "Shall we fight our way through this swamp on a straight northeast course or follow the stream out to the main river?"

"Why don't we give it a try," Roy added, "on a northeast course and if it gets too deep or too thick, we can always head toward the stream."

Everyone was in agreement and off they twisted and splashed. "That was a close one!" Brian exclaimed, wiping the sweat off his forehead with his wet sleeve.

Irwin was trudging just behind and added, "Sure was a good thing we had that escape trail, for we'd likely never have gotten through that bunch of Indians."

Brian was glad that the escape trail had proved to be worth the extra work required to make it. "Thank You, Lord," he prayed silently, "for the revival we experienced in camp a few nights ago. If it weren't for that, we wouldn't be here now, and very likely this tribe wouldn't be reached with the Gospel for many years."

As Brian fought his way through the tangled mass, he was disappointed with the poor reception the savages had given them, yet he was thrilled with the fellowship he was now having with the men. Would this remain? Or would he and Irwin clash again on a later issue? What would Mr. Weatherton say when he heard about the changes?

CHAPTER NINE

The men sloshed their way through the swamp for about four hours and eventually reached the high ground where the camp was. Later in the day, as the sun hid its face behind the horizon, Irwin built the campfire in front of the log cabin. Against the cabin, on a couple of benches they had built, the five men sat relaxing. Guns were propped near by. Down at the river's edge the frogs were croaking happily. Bats were flapping busily as they sought their nightly quota of mosquitos and other insects. The men sang again before discussing the day's events and plans for the morrow.

After the missionaries had sung awhile and praised the Lord for His protection, Irwin spoke. "Let's decide what our tactics should be in the days ahead. Why don't you give your ideas first, Brian?"

Brian stared into the crackling fire. Roy and Jim were sitting beside him. On the other bench sat Irwin and Dick. "It's hard to say what our next approach should be," he began slowly, leaning forward and resting his arm on his legs. "It's certain the savages don't like us around. Nevertheless, I'm convinced that God wants us to reach these souls with the Gospel message." He lowered both hands to the bench to lift himself and shift his weight.

"The savages know we're around now, so there's no point in going into the jungle where the risk is great. I suggest we take the canoe the two turns upriver to where our trail begins and keep putting out gifts. We could also put out some gifts around the camp. It would be best to stay on the north side of the river when we go back and forth, out of the reach of the arrows, in case some of those boys get string-happy again. Other than that we might just as well hang around camp and wait for them to eventually come around."

Everyone discussed Brian's suggestions and the entire group agreed with him. Irwin added, "I noticed on the aerial photos that there's a good-sized stretch of grassland north across the river about half a mile. What do you fellas think of the idea of making a good wide trail over to the campo and building the airstrip we were talking about before? Making one from cleared jungle would be a stupendous job."

"Sounds good," Roy said, getting up to stretch and to add a couple more pieces of wood to the fire. "If Mike could come in on land, he could carry a lot more cargo, making the cost much less."

"We could make a couple of wheelbarrows," Brian added, hitting a mosquito on the back of his neck, "and that would make it easier to carry cargo from the airstrip."

Dick spoke in his Tennessee drawl. "Let's go upriver every morning after breakfast and check the gifts. After that we can work on our trail to the pampa. Then we can come back about five o'-clock and check the gifts upriver again before taking baths and eating."

Brian felt an inner glow of satisfaction, for it was refreshing to talk things over as a group and to reach an agreement pleasing to everyone. Because of this unity and oneness in prayer and concern for a friendly contact, he was certain that the Lord would soon work in the hearts of the savages, changing their hostile attitude.

Weeks passed with no sign of the Indians. No one could figure out why the savages didn't come to the main river to take the gifts or attempt to drive the missionaries away from their camp. The wide path was made to the pampa and after several more days of work the men cleared the grass, ant hills and brush until the airstrip was completed. There were enough supplies on hand so no flight had been requested since Brian and Irwin had come back.

Finally, about two months afterward, the five headed upriver for their daily check. Dick was at the front of the boat, alert as always and holding his shotgun erect. As Irwin turned the outboard motor to cross over to the little clearing, Dick shouted, "Hey, the gifts are gone."

The men hurried to shore and up the embankment. A new thrill raced through Brian's veins as he inspected the spot where the gift had been taken. In place of it was a wad of leaves with small vines wrapped around like a roll of yarn. "What in the world do you suppose this junk means?" he asked, looking it over.

Each man inspected it and gave a guess regarding the Indians' purpose in hanging the strange object. More gifts were hung—hard corn in a large tin can as well as another ax and a couple of strands of beads.

In a few days, as hope and excitement ran high among the missionaries, one of the gift knives at the south end of the camp clearing was missing. It had been agreed that when the savages came out, one man would stay in the log cabin with a gun, ready to shoot into the air should it be necessary. The others would stay close by and unarmed.

Several days in a row the gifts were taken. Brian sensed that the savages were spying for hours at a time. Then in the middle of one afternoon the men jumped up from their activities. "What was that?" Irwin asked, turning his head sideways and motioning to the others to be silent.

"Sounds like the savages are chanting over at the south end of the clearing!" Roy exclaimed, straining to hear better.

Brian buckled on his gunbelt and said with excitement in his voice, "Let's go part of the way over and motion for them to come in. How about taking some gifts along?"

Four men walked cautiously toward the edge of the clearing. Irwin was in the lead. Dick stayed back at the cabin with his shotgun ready and his pouch filled with extra shells. Irwin and Brian held the gifts over their heads, beckoning with their free hands for the unseen Indians to come out and accept their presents. Brian could feel his heart pounding in his chest. "This is about as far as we should go. Let's keep out of the range of arrows."

"Yeah, I agree with you," Irwin said with a tense voice.

The four men stood for more than fifteen minutes calling and waving.

"I've got an idea," Brian said, keeping his eyes on the jungle's edge. "I'm single and more expendable. Maybe it'd be best if the three of you went back to the cabin and I stood here alone for awhile. That might encourage them to come out and accept our gifts." The savages continued to chant in a weird minor tone.

"I don't know," Irwin began with uncertainty in his voice. "I'd sure hate to see anything happen to you."

"If anything happens or they start shooting arrows, I guarantee I'll break my own high school record on the hundred-yard dash," Brian assured him.

"What do the rest of you men think?" the assistant director asked.

Roy spoke. "We're not getting anywhere this way so why not take a chance?" Jim agreed so the three backed off toward the cabin.

Brian's heart continued to pound as he held up the ax and motioned. There was a movement in the brush so he put one foot forward to be ready to push himself off to a running start should arrows start to fly. The chanting intensified farther back in the dense jungle. Finally a young warrior stepped partly out from behind a large tree. A new thrill tingled every nerve as Brian stared at the savage. His hair was long and he too was chanting and spitting. A small black goatee jutted from his light-brown chin. Brian motioned to him to come, then took a couple of steps forward.

"The poor fella," he thought. "He looks so terrified. He must surely wonder if we're going to get revenge for the times they attacked us."

In a few minutes the frightened Indian stepped farther out, exposing his muscular naked body. He kept motioning for Brian to come to him. The distance between them was nearly two hundred feet. Brian cautiously closed the space by nearly half and as he stopped he motioned to the young brown man to come the other half of the way.

The air was tense and it seemed as if all nature were holding its breath as two opposite cultures faced each other. The savage folded his arms upward in front of his chest with his fists nearly under his chin. Brian thought this might be a gesture to protect himself. The terrified warrior took a step forward, then another. Slowly he came toward Brian, now leaning forward and extending one arm. The white man, perspiring profusely, extended his arm. Finally the savage took the ax and hurried back into hiding. The chanting stopped and Brian concluded that the savages had left.

He pulled out his handkerchief and wiped his brow. Suddenly, as he headed back to the log cabin, he realized how tense and tired he was.

"Praise the Lord!" the men exclaimed as Brian drew near.

"A tremendous victory!" Irwin said, smiling broadly.

Brian sat down on the bench with excitement still surging through his veins. He had felt like this when he took his first roller-coaster ride. "This is hard on the heart," he said kiddingly.

He reported the news on the regular four-thirty P.M. radio contact with the base and could hear Mike give a big "Whooooopeeee."

It was Roy's turn to cook supper so he started the fire and washed the rice. Everyone was too excited to do much more than sit and talk. Soon the conversation concerned what they should do when more Indians came out, whether they should give them gifts or try as soon as possible to get them to trade, so as to learn values.

"One of the first things we ought to do," Brian proposed convincingly, "is to show these savages what our guns can do. That way they'll respect us and won't try to pull anything later."

"In what way do you mean?" Roy asked as he straightened himself from stirring the soup he had put on the fire beside the rice.

"Let's take one of our empty five-gallon kerosene cans and tell the Indians we're going to shoot it with Dick's shotgun. When they see it full of holes, it should be persuasive." Brian looked at Irwin, figuring he would go along with the suggestion, then added, "What do you think, boss?"

"Boy, I don't know," Irwin said as his face clouded with perplexity. "If you ask me, we're asking for trouble by shooting too soon."

"It was done successfully in the recent contact in Bolivia," Brian said defensively. Suddenly he wondered if this point of argument would cause antagonism between him and Irwin. Brian thought for a moment, considering the problem. Was this principle important enough to defend, or should he surrender the idea and thus preserve the harmony he had recently achieved with Irwin? He wondered what his answer should be. His thoughts were interrupted when he heard Irwin speak again.

"It troubles me to think we still have to lean on physical means to make spiritual gains. I realize that in the past I went to extremes in thinking that God would work things out without the instrumentality of man or things. But now are we going to the other extreme?"

Brian could sense agitation in Irwin's voice. "Let's face it, no matter what we do or what methods we use, we're still helpless if God doesn't protect and care for us. We can influence their thinking by something they can see and I believe that God uses such means."

Irwin drew in his lips and raised his eyebrows. "Maybe we'd better drop the subject to avoid friction."

"I suggest we pray about it," Brian said with a grave look in his eyes, "and then discuss the subject later, for the proper solution to this problem may even save our lives later on."

"Let's eat, men." Roy urged, after licking the hot soup from the wooden spoon. "Tastes pretty good, even if I have to brag about my own cooking."

Brian laughed. "You can't kid me, buddy. That's boughten soup mix. We'll have to give the factory the credit."

"O.K.," Roy said, feigning a hurt look. "I could have burned it."

"All right." Brian teased. "We'll give you half the credit and the factory the other half."

The following day, as the men were sitting on the logs or benches with their bowls of oatmeal in their hands, the chanting began again just beyond the clearing. The men went into action. First they took the few clothes off the line and locked them inside the log cabin. Jim went inside to the second floor to observe and stand guard. Dick said he would stay outside the cabin with his gun. Brian, Irwin and Roy walked slowly through the shaded area to where Brian had stood the day before. The three beckoned to the savages to come out and receive the gifts.

After much coaxing, five husky savages cautiously stepped out a couple of feet into the clearing and motioned for the three white men to come to them. Brian could see other savages peering from behind trees and clumps of brush with their bows and arrows ready. The five light-brown men were obviously afraid as they took the gifts from the missionaries. For more than half an hour they jabbered and gestured and the white men finally realized that the savages wanted more knives and axes.

"We'd better not give them too many," Irwin suggested, "or we'll never be able to carry out our principle of trading.

"Right," Brian replied as he motioned to the savages in an attempt to show them that he wanted one of their bows and arrows, and that in return he would go the the cabin and bring another gift. Apparently, however, they did not understand so nothing happened. Roy slipped away and brought back a few ears of dried corn. The Indians accepted it readily.

Five more days of contact passed similarly. Each time the savages, sometimes as many as twenty, came closer toward the cabin. One day one of the more outspoken Indians whom the missionaries dubbed "Gimme," demanded that Brian go to the cabin and bring him an ax. He wouldn't take "no" for an answer. "I want to show you something," Brian said to Gimme, knowing of course that he didn't understand.

Brian went back to the log cabin and called to Jim inside. "Keep alert, buddy; there might be trouble as these Indians are getting more demanding and nasty."

"Yeah," Jim shouted back. "I noticed it. Maybe it's a good time to give a gun demonstration."

"That's what I came for. I was thinking the same thing," Brian said as Dick handed him the shotgun and a couple of extra shells. Then he picked up the shiny kerosene can and walked slowly toward the middle of the clearing, watching closely for any reaction the savages might have to his carrying a gun. The ten Indians, milling around excitedly, had left their bows and arrows hidden in the jungle as the missionaries had insisted from the beginning that they not bring them out.

When he had gone part of the distance, Brian laid the can on the ground and continued to walk slowly toward the group. He approached the curly-haired Indian who appeared to be the chief. Using sign language, he explained to the broad-shouldered, long-haired man that he was going to go "boom-boom" at the can. The other savages closed in as he explained several times what he was going to do. He wanted to prepare them, thoroughly. Then, stepping forward, he raised the gun. *Wham!* Brian looked back to see five men dash for cover. About twenty other warriors stepped out from their jungle hiding places with their bows and arrows in readiness. The chief's eyes nearly jumped from their sockets and his jaw dropped in amazement. Brian laughed heartily to show them he wasn't angry and had no evil intentions. Irwin and Roy understood his purpose and laughed loudly also, pointing at the can to show the remaining five Indians that it was a harmless demonstration.

While Brian walked over to get the can, both Roy and Irwin tried to tell the savages that the gun, like their bows and arrows, was used to shoot animals and birds. Again amazement etched deeper lines into the chief's forehead as he raised his eyebrows and inspected the twenty holes in the can. A little later the other five savages, including Gimme, came back into the clearing. Others who had stepped out into the clearing, ready to use their bows and arrows, had gone back to their hiding places.

Shortly two parrots landed in a high tree near the bank of the river. The chief pointed to them and said, "boom-boom." Brian sneaked slowly in the direction of the birds and shot. Both came down with a thud. Throwing the strap of the gun over his shoulder, he picked up the bright blue and yellow parrots and presented them to the chief. The Indian's eyes lit up as he pulled out the tail feathers and gave the birds to a younger warrior with the instruction that he take them away into the jungle.

During the days following, the savages became friendlier. Neither Gimme nor any of the others made harsh demands as they had done before. After nearly two weeks of friendly contacts, a cold south wind roared in, which happens frequently during the dry season. The Indians headed back to their village, but said in sign language that they would be back in about ten sleeps.

Since supplies were low a list of needed provisions was given to Mike by radio so that he could bring them. Excitement ran high the day of the flight. There was still a south wind of about twenty-five miles an hour and the dark clouds, about two thousand feet high, were still rolling past. About half an hour before the pilot was due in, the five men locked the log cabin, closed the window shutters and took off across the river and on down the trail to the airstrip.

"Just what sort of news will the mail bring?" Brian wondered as he zigzagged over the jungle trail. "It's been several weeks now with no mail. I wonder what June will say in her letters."

CHAPTER TEN

After all the supplies had been brought from the airstrip to the river by means of the two homemade wheelbarrows, the men loaded the provisions into the canoe to bring them to the other side. They appreciated the cool, cloudy day for working. After everything had been stashed away safely inside the log cabin, Irwin opened the box that contained the mail. He distributed it piece by piece until it was gone.

"But why only one letter from June?" Brian thought depressingly as he climbed the stairs to read his mail while he sat on the edge of his cot. Roy was upstairs, too. The others went outside to read. When Brian tore the envelope open he noticed that Roy had received three letters from June. "Just what is going on here?" he wondered.

He read the short letter from June and it seemed as if his mind went temporarily blank as the blood drained from his face. Roy looked up from reading and stared a moment at him. "What in the world happened to you? You look like you saw a ghost and are about ready to fight him," Roy said in wonderment.

Brian shook his head as he stared at the floor. He was too choked with emotion to speak. Finally he said, "June has called it off between us." He spoke dejectedly.

"Don't tell me!" his friend returned with heaviness in his tone. "I figured that was sewed up for good. Did she say why?"

"She didn't give any reason at all. Besides that she said she's going back to the States to study leprosy."

Roy laid his letters down. "Leprosy! It doesn't make sense. She worked in the general hospital six months to complete her study of tropical diseases and now she's going into leprosy study. Our mission doesn't even have a leper colony."

"I know," Brian returned slowly. "There's something fishy about this whole deal."

"I got three letters from her, which was a surprise to me," Roy said as he pulled them out from the pile of letters. "Maybe she has more news in these."

Brian waited as Roy read silently. He thought, *I bet Mr. Weatherton is sending her to the States to make sure I don't go with her. No doubt he's poisoned her mind against me and she thinks I'm a rascal, a troublemaker, a good-for-nothing missionary. Maybe I should have told her how God worked through me in saving Irwin's life. Her father still doesn't know these things; if Irwin wrote contrary to what he'd written before, Mr. Weatherton hasn't gotten the letter, for it just went out today with Mike.* Hatred seethed within him. *Lord, I admit,* he prayed silently, *that once again there's real bitterness and hatred in my heart toward the director. This isn't of You; it's wrong. I need Your help to get rid of it. I . . .*

"She doesn't give any reason in these letters either," Roy added, unknowingly interrupting Brian's praying. "She writes a lot of news about various people and mentions how she enjoyed the times we played Scrabble together and so on."

"Sounds like she's getting a liking for you," Brian said, looking up at his buddy.

"If she is, it isn't because I've made a play for her. You know that, don't you?" Roy asked.

"Yeah, I know. You've been real fair in keeping your hands off, you handsome brute," Brian said, forcing a smile. "I guess all is fair and square in love and you can go after her now if you want to."

"She sure is a beauty, but I have some real doubts about her. Maybe you're better off . . ." Roy stopped abruptly.

"Better off what?"

"I don't want to say for I don't want to hurt your feelings any more than they have been." Roy offered.

"Can't be any worse, buddy. Come out with it."

"I was going to say that maybe you're better off not going with her. It might help your relations with the director. And you might have found out too late that she wasn't the type you need for a wife."

Brian sighed and opened the letter from his father. He would have to think this thing through after he had read all the letters and could be alone. Another pain shot through him as he read, "Your mother had a stroke yesterday and we had to take her to the hospital. For the present she is paralyzed on her left side, but the doctor seems to think she will be over this in a little while." He looked at the date on the letter. It had been written two weeks before. *I wonder how Mom is doing now,* he thought. *That's the difficulty of living beyond civilization: it takes so long to get mail in and out,* he reflected.

The following morning, after Irwin had shouted for the men to get up, Brian slipped from under his mosquito net and sat with his chin in his cupped hands.

"Still feeling pretty badly about the whole deal?" Roy asked with compassion.

"Yeah, it bugs me." He spoke disgustedly. "I wish in many ways I could be out on the base to talk things over with June and her dad."

"The Lord knows. It might be just as well you're right here," his friend said consolingly. "There must be a reason for all of this."

Brian felt the chill of the morning. A slight south wind was still blowing the heavy gray clouds. It felt good to put on a warm sweater. The men ate breakfast inside the cabin to keep out of the chilling wind. During the meal the men exchanged news from various parts of the country and from home. Brian listened silently with a heavy heart. As he was about to finish his coffee, Irwin looked at his watch.

"Radio time, Brian," Irwin said pleasantly.

He reached over and flipped the switch to warm up the set. For a few minutes Mike talked with a missionary in another tribal area. Then he heard him call the Panube camp number.

"This is CPF95N," Brian began. "Do you have anything this morning for us? Over."

"Howdy, Brian. We have only one item. There is a cable here for you from Oregon. Would you like me to open it and let you know what it says? Over."

"O.K., Mike, go ahead. Over." There was a pause, and a chill went up his back as the first thought that came to his mind concerned what he had read in his father's letter.

"Here's what it says: 'Mother died suddenly of heart attack. Stop. If you can come, money is deposited in checking account. Stop. Dad.'" There was a silence for a moment and then Mike continued. "I'm sure sorry about this news. Do you want me to make a flight in there to bring you out? Over."

"Give me a call at eight o'clock and I'll let you know. Over."

Brian poured himself another cup of coffee and sat down at the table. Each of the men expressed his deepest sympathy and promised that he would pray for him and for his father, brothers and sisters.

"You've got a perfect right to go to the States if you want to," Irwin said with hurt showing in his eyes. "I'm sure we can hold the fort here until you can make it back."

"Thanks, Irwin," Brian said, staring into his coffee. "I appreciate your considerations. I was just debating the pros and cons. If it were my father who had passed away, I would owe it to my mother to help and comfort her and to square things away, but I know Dad can get along all right. I'd still like to be there for the funeral but I don't think it's vital. In many ways I'd rather remember Mom as I last saw her, with her sweet, smiling face and in good health.

A few minutes later Brian sent a message on the radio. "Mike, I don't think I'll come out. However, please write down this message and send this cable to my father." Mike said he'd send the cable right away expressing Brian's sympathies.

There was nothing planned for the day except to write letters or do whatever one wanted to do. Since the contacts the missionaries had agreed to hunt on the other side of the river. Brian asked Dick for the use of his gun as he wanted to go to the airstrip, where he could read the Word, pray and think. If an animal or a bird came across his path, he would enjoy bringing it back to camp for it would be a welcome change from the canned meat. "There's a lot to think about," he mumbled as he got into the canoe to go to the other side. "There's June. Mr. Weatherton. And possible discipline from the mission. And Mom . . ."

Out on the airstrip, at the edge of the jungle, Brian looked up. The sky was still leaden with dark clouds. There was no one around to see him give vent to his emotions. His heart was heavy with sorrow for the two loved ones who had now gone from his life. Tears flooded his eyes and coursed freely down his cheeks. He had never known this kind of sorrow, and it had been many years since he had wept so freely. "June," he cried, knowing no one was listening, "why did you leave me? I was sure your love for me was deep and real. If you have come to believe, through your father, that I'm a troublemaker, why couldn't you check into the situation more thoroughly? June, love endures long; is never envious; never boils over with jealousy; is ever ready to believe the best of every person.

June, it tears my heart to know you are leaving Brazil and that I may never see you again. Oh, how heavy my heart is! I remember your beautiful dark eyes and soft hair. Your lips—how waves of happiness rolled over me when your soft, tender lips touched mine! Now I'll never touch them again. How can I stand the thought of your going out of my life?"

Suddenly he wondered, "Are you the cause of all this, Mr. Weatherton?" As this thought flashed into his mind the fountain of tears dried up and his sorrow turned to resentment and anger. "I've prayed for you and have tried to do everything possible without compromise to win your friendship and to work in harmony. You've constantly misunderstood me, never cared to investigate thoroughly to see what was the truth. You think I'm too low-down to be seen with your daughter. I thought there was hope when you admitted you were allowing yourself to be so busy that you failed to spend the proper time in prayer. Now it looks as if you've done nothing about this conviction, and this is hurting me all the more. And hurting yourself, too. You've broken up my love relationship with June and I hate you for it. I know this is wrong and I don't want to hate, yet it seems to overwhelm me. I'm sure I'll get over it, confess my wrong feelings and be forgiven by God, but at this moment it's very alive in my heart. You even threaten to dismiss me, leaving me a man without a mission board, thus hindering my ministry and causing me to go through the future with this unjust stigma.

"Oh, God, is there any use in going on? Will You allow one man to wreck my future? Will You not come to my rescue? In time of need why do You remain silent? Does my sin of bitterness and hatred make the heavens as brass? Lord, You know I've confessed this wrong to You and I do again. You know I've tried to make it right with Mr. Weatherton but he put me off. Must I go on carrying this heavy load? Give me a chance to forgive the director and to be forgiven. Oh, God, help me in this dark hour.

"Mother, I'm glad you're in the presence of your Lord and Saviour. Yet my heart aches for your loss. You went early—you were only sixty years old. Who will take your place in interceding for me? Who will take the time to pray and move the hand of God in my behalf? I'm on the very verge of calling it quits because there are no other intercessors who move the hand of God, thus giving me encouragement and hope. I know Dad prays, but he doesn't have the time you had, Mom. Mother, you've been so dear and precious to me. I remember your tears as I left to come to Brazil. You said you would miss me and maybe never see me again here on earth, but you said, 'Son, I've given you to Jesus. Go with my blessing.' That meant so much to me, Mother, to know that the work of the Lord came before your own desires to have me near by."

Again the tears flowed freely down the face of the lonely and crushed missionary as he sat on a log with the jungle behind him and the open grassland before. The battle raged on in his heart. Never before had he experienced such a crisis, such a temptation to quit, to resign in order to save face and escape the stigma that would cling to him the rest of his life. Could one continue successfully when there was constant opposition? No one, except God, would ever know the chaos of emotions and thoughts within him. No one, except God, would ever know that the crushed missionary wept bitter tears. Those things are never told, not even to closest friends. Neither Roy nor the other men in camp would ever know the battle that was fought out there more than half a mile away. These were experiences that only a missionary could know. His sorrow had nearly overpowered his desire to reach those who had never heard the story of salvation.

He sat in silence. Time seemed to be without measure as there were no schedules to meet, no deadlines for accomplishing a certain amount of work. Even the sun was hidden and could not reveal the time of day, and Brian did not think to look at his wrist watch.

Earthly sorrows and troubles began to fade as his eyelids became heavy with sleep. He seemed to be carried away and all feelings and emotions faded into the eternal past. Was this a dream or was it real? He looked down from a great height and saw a tiny speck of a man brokenhearted, on the edge of the grassland. He wanted to shout to him to cheer him, for the human tongue could not describe what he was experiencing. It was glorious. He wanted to tell that little man that life's trials are nothing in comparison with the glory revealed in the saints who are with the Lord. "Oh, that's I down there. How could I possibly be sorrowing when God has made such wonderful provision for victory over sin, self and the powers of darkness? I must go back there and touch that small, insignificant man. Oh, that's right—it's I down there. How confusing!"

A couple of screaming parrots flew over. Brian shook his head. "I must have been dreaming. It seemed as if I were past all of this distress and over in glory, beholding the wonders that God has prepared for those that love Him." His heart was lighter. Did the Lord send him this dream at this time? He didn't believe that dreams in this age are significant, but at least this one had made him feel better.

He opened his Bible and read several comforting Psalms. Then he turned to the Book of Acts and marveled how Paul and Silas could sing as their hands and feet were fast in stocks in the inner prison. Their backs were bloody from the beatings they had received. Yet they were singing at midnight. *Sure, I know why they could sing,* he thought. *In spite of their circumstances and unjust treatment, they could rejoice in the fact that Jesus dwelt within by His Holy Spirit. All right, Lord, take control of my life once again so I can sing within and let the expression flow outward.*

"I know You led me thus far, Lord," he prayed. "Every step of the way You gave the inner assurance that You were leading. Forgive me, Lord, for even considering giving up. Jesus didn't give up and come down from the cross. My troubles don't even begin to compare with His suffering."

He looked at his watch. It was eleven-thirty A.M. so he prepared to go back to camp. His legs were stiff from several hours of sitting. Slinging the shotgun over his shoulder, he started walking slowly, hoping to see a wild turkey on the way. The men had seen plenty of them, but they had agreed not to do any shooting. The path was like a tunnel through the dense, moldy jungle. One could scarcely get lost for he couldn't get off the trail without effort. How much lighter his heart was now than when he had traveled this pathway a few hours before. He was grateful he could be alone to analyze his emotions and expose them to the Lord. The fast pace of living at home, he reasoned, made it extremely difficult for one to do as Scripture exhorted: "Be still, and know that I am God."

He reached the river. The smell of smoke suddenly made him feel hungry so he hurried across.

"Hi, Brian," Irwin called as he pulled a couple of sticks away from the fire so that the food would cook more slowly. "Did you see anything to shoot at?"

"Every living creature must have heard me traipsing through and taken off in fright. Nearly every step I took, a twig would snap underneath." Brian grinned as he laid the gun against the cabin. "Dinner about ready?"

"Yeah," Irwin replied, "as soon as Dick and Jim come back from fishing at the sandbar. You're looking much happier than when you left. You must have had a good time with the Lord."

"I feel much better," Brian confided. "Some of the news I got in the last mail, besides that cable about Mom, just about sent me for a loop, so I just had to get alone and talk things over with the Lord."

"I assure you I'll do everything I can to clear things up between you and Mr. Weatherton. I wrote him quite a while ago but he just got the letter when the plane went back," Irwin said, sympathy evident in his voice.

"I appreciate that, Irwin," Brian said, wondering if it would help, since severe damage had already been done. He had fully forgiven Irwin for what he had said, done and written before. *It's too bad,* Brian thought, *that damage can't be undone the moment sin is confessed to God and to the one wronged.*

He went upstairs to read the other mail again. He had already glanced through several of the letters but the disturbing news from June had made him forget their contents. However, as he opened Evelyn's letter again, he remembered that it had been an encouragement.

". . . and another thing I wanted to write you about is to let you know how happy I've been in the Lord. Since the Lord delivered me from demon harassment by giving you wisdom and then using you to help me, I can't praise Him enough for the power there is in His Name and blood. As you asked me to let you know how things are going, I can say that the devil had often tried to bring the depression back on me but I did as you suggested. I just told him, in the Name of Jesus, to leave me alone, and it worked. These verses have been a real help: 'Submit yourselves therefore to God. Resist the devil, and he will flee from you' (James 4:7). '. . . Be strong in the Lord, and in the power of his might. Put on the whole armour of God, that ye may be able to stand against the wiles of the devil' (Eph. 6:10-11).

"I've had a real burden of prayer lately for you men. One morning at the breakfast table, when Mr. Weatherton asked for prayer requests, I asked that we pray especially for you men as somehow I had unrest in my heart. Several prayed. You can imagine our thrill when we heard on the radio that afternoon how the Lord delivered you men from the Indian ambush."

Brian laid the letter down. "That sure sounds like my mother," he thought. "What a tremendous blessing to have friends who are sensitive to the leading and voice of the Lord!" He continued to read.

"If any of you men have special prayer requests, be sure and send them along and I'll pray daily and present your needs at our prayer meetings here. Mr. Weatherton asked me to stay at the base awhile to do his secretarial work until he can get a replacement. I'm sure you've heard that June is going back to the States for further study. No doubt you are saddened by the thought that you will not be able to see her before she leaves."

Her letter contained other items of news that were of interest to Brian. However, before he finished reading he heard Irwin shout that dinner was ready. Brian slipped down the crude steps and went outside. Dick and Jim were smiling broadly.

"Hi, Brian. We brought you a minnow for your supper," Jim said mischievously.

"Wow!" He exclaimed as he saw the huge fish which the men had caught. "You must have had a terrific fight to land him. How much does it weigh?"

"Dunno," Dick said. "Guess maybe at least seventy pounds. We thought we'd put him on a bigger hook to see if we can catch the bigger one that got away."

That brought laughter. Brian had heard that there were huge catfish in most of these rivers, but this was the first he had seen. It was a good five feet long and had stripes similar to those of a tiger, except for the fact that they were gray and black.

"Let's throw out Irwin's grub and start all over with a fish fry," he suggested, winking. Irwin dished out the food and while the fellows ate they retold how they had caught the fish.

"Did I tell you men that I got a letter from Mr. Weatherton and he said that in about a month he'd like to pay us a visit?" Brian asked. He didn't tell them the director had written that he had several matters to discuss with Brian. *By the way,* he wondered, *just why would he want to make an expensive trip primarily to talk to me?*

CHAPTER ELEVEN

Another month had slipped by rapidly. The rainy season was due. Already there had been a few tropical storms. It was the day for Mike to fly in with Mr. Weatherton. The work had been going well as the missionaries had made several encouraging contacts with the savages. For a period of two weeks thirty to forty Indians had come out every day. The men were progressing well in their study of the language and had been amazed by the success of the contact. There had been several tense moments but when Dick had picked up his gun the naked savages had gotten the point and behaved.

It was seven-thirty A.M., time for the morning contact with the base. The sky was bright blue with glistening fluffy clouds scattered about. Then Brian heard Mike's voice.

"CPX27N calling CPF95N. Are you on? Over."

Brian pushed on the microphone button. "This is CPF95N. We're on, Mike. What do you have? Over."

"O.K.," the friendly voice answered, "we'll be leaving about eleven A.M. to come up your way. How's the weather? Over."

Brian gave the weather report. Mike asked him to come on again at eleven o'clock for another weather report and then to stand by every fifteen minutes for reports while the pilot was flying.

The weather still looked good when Brian reported at eleven o'clock so Mike said he and Mr. Weatherton would leave immediately. Every fifteen minutes Brian jotted down the information Mike gave him regarding their location. At twelve-thirty P.M. Mike called again as Irwin, Dick and Jim were getting ready to head out for the airstrip.

"Brian, are you on?" Mike called.

"Standing by. Over," he said into the microphone.

"How's the weather there?"

"It's a bit more cloudy but there's quite a bit of blue sky. What's up? Over." Brian wrinkled his forehead in apprehension.

"Up ahead of me are a lot of big thunderheads. They look kinda ugly. I'll see if I can go around them. Over."

"Standing by."

Brian ran to the edge of the bank as the three men were about to shove off with the canoe. "You guys want to take my transistor radio? Mike just said there are some bad clouds ahead, so he might have to go back yet. If you have my radio, you'll know if he turns back and you won't have to wait at the airstrip wondering."

"Good idea," Dick shouted in reply as he climbed out of the boat. He returned to the cabin to get Brian's radio.

Roy was outside building a huge fire so there would be plenty of smoke later when the plane was due.

"Brian," Mike called again ten minutes later, "I don't know if I'm going to make it. The storm is too widespread to go around it. I'm going to try and go down to two thousand feet to see if I can fly under the clouds. It's already pretty bumpy. I'll be back in a couple of minutes. I . . ." Brian heard a terrific clap of thunder. "That was close. Over."

Brian stood by, feeling his muscles tense. Roy sat near him, waiting intently for Mike to come back on.

"This is CP635, Brian. The weather is too severe. I'm turning back right now. Lightning is striking all over and I'm down to one thousand feet with visibility at zero. I should be out of it in a few minutes. I'm now heading due south. There's . . ."

Suddenly, with a squeal, the radio went dead. Brian turned to Roy with a tense look. "Sounds like a tube went out."

"Yeah." Roy spoke in a hushed voice. "I'm just wondering if lightning hit the plane and burned out his radio. I wonder if . . ." Roy said no more. Brian knew what he was thinking.

"I'll give the plane another call. It may be hard to hear them now as the static is quite loud," Brian said as he pressed the button.

"CP635. CP635. Mike, if you can hear me, turn your set off and on so I'll know you're O.K. It sounded like you burned a tube. Over." The two men listened intently for a signal. They could hear only static.

"CPX27N. This is CPF95N calling. I can't hear anything more from the plane. Are you reading me and could you hear anything from CP635? Over."

Mike's wife came on. "It's hard reading you as we have a lot of static. I can't pick up the plane any more. I heard him say he had to turn back because of the weather but that's the last information I got. Over."

"O.K., Myrna." Brian spoke loudly. "It sounded like his radio burned out. Let's see . . . he should be arriving back about two-fifteen. Let's come on at that time for a check. Over."

In half an hour the other three men came back from the airstrip as they had heard Mike say on the radio that he had been forced to turn back. "Doesn't sound too good," Irwin remarked as he reached the top of the embankment and walked to the cabin.

The men ate their dinner in silence. Brian knew that they were thinking and wondering just as he was. Was the plane still flying? The minutes dragged like hours as the men waited for the radio contact at two-fifteen P.M. Finally it came and Brian called in. Myrna, Mike's young wife, said he hadn't returned yet so they agreed to come on every fifteen minutes.

"I imagine that with the load he was carrying he couldn't fly more than five and a half hours," Irwin said as his face clouded with anxiety. "That means if he had to do a lot of zigzagging around he'd have to be in before four-thirty. Out here in the jungle there aren't any alternate places to fly to."

Two-thirty P.M. came and went and still the plane had not returned to the base. Two-forty-five, three, three-fifteen, and still no sign of the plane.

At four-thirty in the afternoon there was still no trace so Brian made arrangements for a radio broacast at nine P.M. to discuss plans. In the meantime the missionaries would consider a possible course of action.

Supper was early and before dark the men built a fire and seated themselves on logs, facing each other.

"There seems to be no doubt," Irwin began gravely, "that the plane either crashed or had to make a forced landing somewhere. Those first storms of the rainy season are really severe. If he was just half an hour from here, that would mean he was very likely over the grassland." The men gathered around Irwin as he unfolded a map. "If they went down over the campo, I'd say they had a good chance of making a forced landing without getting banged up too much."

"Even though there are no trees, those ant and termite hills could tear off the landing gear in a hurry," Roy added.

"One thing is for sure," Brian said. "They'd never put that plane down in one piece. When we made our airstrip I was surprised to see how many of those hard ant hills there were."

"The plane is closer to us," Irwin began, laying the map aside as the others seated themselves again. "We'll have to go after them. But that swamp—I don't know if we'll be able to get through it."

"We'll have to give it a try," Brian said with seriousness in his voice. "We've got to make it, in fact."

Roy kicked a stick farther into the fire, then spoke. "I suggest that two men go and three stay here because the savages may be out again and we can't leave the camp abandoned."

"Maybe we should draw straws," Jim suggested.

"It'd be fair enough but if you men would permit it, I'd like to go, in the worst way," Brian said. "Not that I'm adventurous or eager to go through that swamp, but if Mr. Weatherton is alive, I've got to clear my heart with him. I mentioned to you men the other day about my difficulty with him, and I'll never know full joy and peace in my heart until I can talk with him and get some things squared away."

"We ought to give Brian the opportunity to go," Irwin agreed. "I'd be willing to go with him unless one of you men would like to go for some reason."

Dick looked up from doodling in the dirt with a stick. "I'm sure we all would be willing to take the tremendous risks involved to reach the plane, and I sure wouldn't want anyone to think I'd pass the buck. Nevertheless I feel that Brian and Irwin should go."

Jim and Roy also agreed to this. Thunder began to rumble and echo in the south as the air became heavy and still. They continued to discuss what medical supplies and food they should take with them.

"I think it will take us about a week to get there," Brian said. It was now pitch dark and the fire cast a yellow glow on every serious face. Lightning lit the camp sporadically with a dazzling blue-white light. "And it'll take us that long just to hack a narrow trail wide enough for us to get through and to find our way back," he added.

"I think it'd be good to have the folks at the base get hold of the Brazilian Air Force and see if they will send out a search plane," Roy advised. They could make some sort of deal to drop supplies if there's anyone alive. Too bad they don't have any helicopters in this neck of the woods. You fellas should take your transistor radio and whatever news we have we'll send to you."

"That sounds good," Irwin returned enthusiastically. "When the pilot spots the plane he can send us information as to where it is and what the compass-reading is from our camp to the wreckage. Otherwise it would be mighty hard to find the wreckage in that huge campo."

At nine o'clock that evening, between claps of thunder and in spite of strong static, there was considerable discussion by radio. There were no men at the base so Myrna said she would contact the Air Force to see what arrangements could be made. The storm broke loose and roared through the trees, drenching the camp. After the broadcast the men spent some time praying as they sat around the rustic hand-hewn table. Soon they slipped off to bed for the tension of the day had exhausted them.

The rain was still hammering away at the aluminum roof when Brian fell into a deep sleep.

Irwin was the first one out of bed and he roused the other men as the eastern sky was beginning to glow. The storm had passed during the night and the sky was clear, but the trees continued to drip as if it were still raining. Brian and Irwin stuffed supplies into their packsacks as Roy prepared breakfast. Often the two men lifted their packs to make sure they were of equal weight.

Brian was jumpy. Nervously he faced the unknown and the uncertainty of what they would find when they reached the scene of the accident. Breakfast was tasteless and difficult to eat as his thoughts wandered.

After prayer the two men struggled into their packsacks and, picking up their machetes, headed off in a southerly direction. Irwin was in the lead and started to cut through the thick brush. Brian carried his compass in one hand and blazed trees with the other. They had been cutting for only a few minutes when the orange sun began to peek through the jungle growth, making the droplets of water sparkle liké jewelry. Already the men were wet from the dripping leaves.

Both Brian and Irwin preferred to wear caps instead of pith helmets when they were in the jungle. A helmet echoed annoyingly and was easily knocked off one's head. Both men started out wearing fairly new denim trousers and work shirts for they knew that thorns and jungle growth would tear their clothing. Inside their packs were tennis shoes which they would wear when walking in the swamp. At four-thirty in the afternoon the perspiring men stopped to rest and Brian dug out his transistor, which had been wrapped carefully in two plastic bags.

Myrna had reported that the Army had sent out a plane but hadn't yet sighted her husband and Mr. Weatherton. She had said they would search every day until they sighted the wreckage. After the broadcast Brian put the small radio back into his packsack.

"Sure hope they spot the wreckage soon," Irwin commented as they shouldered their heavy packs again. "If they don't, we sure won't."

"If the men went down in the campo, I'm sure they'll find them, for a white plane will stand out clearly. Unless . . . unless it burned up." Brian grimaced as he spoke.

As Irwin shifted his straps he added, "Let's continue to hope and pray they're alive. Man, this old pack feels like it's twice as heavy now."

"Mine, too," Brian responded as he ran his thumb under the strap to adjust it. "I declare these straps will cut me in two before long. I didn't think fifty-five pounds could be so heavy."

The men continued to take turns slashing through the dense jungle. About half an hour before dark they stopped cutting trail and cleared a small spot for camp. Brian hurriedly hunted for dry wood while Irwin hung the jungle hammocks. Earlier in the afternoon they had discovered a small creek where they had refilled their canteens. Most of the water would be needed for cooking rice but there would be a little left for drinking.

Shortly after dinner the following day the men were still cutting through the jungle. They were on high ground, although it seemed somewhat soggy. Irwin was cutting and Brian was a few feet behind, now and then chipping off bark from the trees, when suddenly he stood still for a moment.

"Wait a minute, Irwin!" There was silence as Irwin looked puzzled. "Do you hear a plane motor?"

He strained to listen. "Yeah, sure enough! Maybe he found the wreckage and is getting a compass-bearing between it and our camp. Sure hope so!"

"Looks like we're heading in the right direction," Brian said, searching through the tree tops to see if he could see the plane. It passed a little to the east of them and neither was able to catch a glimpse of it.

The missionaries struggled on with new vigor, slashing the green entanglement as they went. Brian was eager for the radio broadcast at 4:30 P.M., so that they could find out if the Army plane had spotted the wreckage and if anyone was alive. When the time finally came he turned the transistor on a few minutes early to make sure they wouldn't miss anything.

"CPF95N. Are you on? This is CPX27N. Over." The feminine voice was full of emotion.

"Right here, Myrna. What's the latest news?" Roy answered from the Panube camp.

"The Army plane got in just a few minutes ago and the pilot spotted our plane. He flew low several times and said one person was outside waving to him. He couldn't tell who he was. The plane was damaged quite a bit. The right wing was torn off and the tail section, too. How do you read me so far? Over."

"Reading you good. Over!" Roy said excitedly.

"O.K. The pilot dropped a note telling our men to stay by the plane as Irwin and Brian are on their way. In the note the pilot also told our men that he would return the next day to drop medicine and food. If you're listening, Brian and Irwin, the pilot said to head a hundred and seventy degrees south. The plane is about two miles south of the edge of the jungle. The Army said they would send in some signal rockets and tell the men that after the fifth day they should shoot one off every hour so that when you come out of the jungle you'll be able to see where to go. We're praying for you men, that you'll be able to make it through the swamp. Do you have anything else, Roy? Over."

After the radio conversation Brian looked up as he began to fold in the antenna. "Praise the Lord they found the wreckage! That's terrific. I'm wondering if one of the men was killed," he said anxiously.

"Since the right wing was torn off it seems that the one sitting on the right side would likely have gotten hurt the most. That would be Mr. Weatherton." Irwin spoke gravely.

The men sat a few minutes in silence, thinking. Their shirts were wet with perspiration. Then Brian got up. "Guess maybe we'd better get at it again. We can go another hour and a half. I wonder how far we've gone."

"Sure would be interesting to know. I'd guess maybe fifteen miles," Irwin said as he slung his heavy pack over his shoulders.

The men labored on, Irwin ahead. They came to a section of jungle where there was very little underbrush and numerous palm trees that spread their fernlike leaves as if clasping hands. The men doubled their pace. Suddenly Brian saw his buddy fall flat on his face and roll to one side with his face twisted in pain. He rushed forward to help him but saw he had fallen into a hole and that his leg was twisted. Hurriedly he slipped the pack off Irwin's back and grasped him firmly under the arms, pulling him away from the hole.

"My knee," Irwin gasped, pain evident in his eyes. "I must have wrenched it."

Brian realized he was still carrying his pack so he removed it and began to inspect Irwin's leg. He dug into his pack for bandages with which to wrap the knee, already beginning to swell, and then adjusted one of the packs so Irwin could lean comfortably against it.

Brian looked at his watch. "Guess maybe we'd better make camp here and then we'll see how you are in the morning. I'll get a fire going and then check around for some water. I wouldn't be surprised if the swamp is just ahead. Here's my revolver in case you need it while I'm gone." He unfastened his gunbelt and laid it beside the stricken man, who was groaning with pain.

Carefully he blazed the trees as he went and after about ten minutes he found water at the edge of the swamp. Gratefully he filled both canteens. Before returning he refreshed himself with a cool bath in the clear water. Back in camp, as the sun was beginning to sink low in the west, Brian hung the two hammocks and tested them to make sure the knots were tight.

After supper Brian helped his friend into his hammock as the injured man found it impossible to move his leg because of the pain. Brian crawled into his hammock to escape the tyranny of the mosquitoes which were hungrily seeking his blood. His muscles ached from swinging a machete all day and the heavy pack had rubbed his flesh raw in several places.

He lay in his hammock, not daring to think what would happen if Irwin couldn't walk. *Maybe he'll be better in the morning, so why think about it?* he reasoned. *Best to wait until morning to see what develops.* He visualized the grassland where Mike, or possibly both of the men, were hungry and thirsty and perhaps in severe pain. Again his thoughts were of June.

I must not think about her now, he reasoned drowsily, *or I'll be so upset I won't be able to sleep.* He conquered these thoughts and soon sleep rescued him from grim realities.

CHAPTER TWELVE

The gray dawn was noisy. As Brian awoke he wondered what was happening. He saw that a few feet away a couple of wild pigs were crunching on palm nuts. When he pulled the zipper that separated the net from the hammock, he heard a couple of snorts as the pigs scooted off.

"How's the leg?" Brian asked, sitting in his hammock with his legs hanging.

"Kept me awake half the night," Irwin said as he shifted in his hammock. "But it doesn't pain so much right now. As soon as you get dressed give me a hand and I'll see if I can walk on it."

Brian clapped his shoes together to make sure they were not sheltering a scorpion and went to help his buddy. Irwin grimaced as he stepped down to the ground and hobbled about, testing his leg.

"Boy, I don't know," he said, shaking his head. "I kinda doubt I'll be able to go very far this way, especially through the swamp ahead."

Brian spoke dejectedly. "Guess we have to face the facts squarely. If you can't make it, you can't make it. What do you think we should do?"

"You go ahead and I'll try to get back the best way I can," Irwin suggested. "Let's put some of the stuff in plastic bags and leave it here hanging in the trees. Maybe later we can get it. Now that an airdrop will be made today there's no point in lugging in all the extra stuff."

"Sounds good," Brian commented, "but I don't like the idea of leaving you alone."

"Those men out by the wreckage are in more desperate need of help than I am. I can make myself a pair of crutches if I have to." He spoke reassuringly as they prepared a supply of extra food, medicine and bedding.

111

"O.K., buddy. I might as well leave the cooking pots here too as there won't be any place to make a fire out in the swamp. I'll just take the raisins and the parched corn and peanut cereal. I suppose I should take some medicine in case they don't drop the right kind." Brian emptied his pack and repacked while the oatmeal was cooking over the fire.

The grayness of the morning brightened and the men wished each other the best. Irwin watched as Brian started off with a lighter pack. A strange feeling of loneliness came over Brian as he began sloshing through ankle-deep water. Fortunately, in the jungle there is much less undergrowth where there is water. As the day wore on the water became deeper and he made blazes higher on the trees. Milky sap oozed from some of the trees immediately and red juice trickled from others.

For the next five days the water was up to his belt. Frequently a slimy log sent his feet from under him and he was drenched. "Sure glad I've got everything wrapped well in plastic bags," he mumbled when he lost his balance and fell. Now and then when a slippery log moved after he had stepped on it, he shivered at the chilling thought that perhaps he had encountered a deadly snake like those about which he had read. He lost no time putting a safe distance between him and the log before he looked back to see if the water was still moving.

Five days of anguish passed as Brian wondered if Mr. Weatherton was alive. *He must be alive,* he often thought. *I've got to see him to clear my heart. Even though he has done me many injustices, I still have no right to harbor this bitterness in my heart toward him.*

"I sure hope I can make it to the campo today," he had groaned as he started out on the fifth day he had spent in the swamp, which was the seventh day since he had left the Panube camp. "I don't have any hammock to sleep in now. I'd have been there all day trying to get those fire-ants off my hammock. I'm sure if I'd tried to get rid of them I'd have been bitten so many times I'd be nutty by now."

He fought on and found it difficult to raise his arms to blaze the trees. His strength was nearly gone. He had not cooked a hot meal or eaten meat for several days and was beginning to feel the effects. He ceased to think about anything in particular. That in itself took energy, he reasoned.

Late in the afternoon, however, the jungle brightened as the trees thinned out. It was a matter of a few hundred yards and he would be on dry ground and the open campo. New energy raced through his veins as he pressed on. He felt his heart pound with excitement and anticipation as he remembered that the Army pilot had reported the wreckage to be about two miles south of the edge of the jungle. Had he kept on a hundred-and-seventy-degree course as he zigzagged for seven days through the jungle and swamp? If he hadn't, Brian was certain he wouldn't know which way to turn when he reached the large open spaces. He wondered how far away the rockets could be seen.

Suddenly the jungle became nearly treeless grassland. The tall grass waved in the hot breeze and Brian squinted in the brightness. Shading his eyes with his cupped hands, he searched the horizon for the orange smoke of a rocket. The minutes ticked away like hours and still there were no signs. His determined jaw dropped in disappointment.

"Lord," he breathed in desperation, looking heavenward, "which way should I go? There's no way to blaze a trail in this grass. Oh, God, what should I do?"

The sun began to lean heavily toward the west. Brian felt desperately alone, heavily burdened physically and spiritually. He was overwhelmed by the vastness of the campo before him and the jungle behind him. Jungle and grassland had no mercy for intruders.

He looked back to the jungle from which he had come. It was hard to see the narrow pathway. He stepped back and cut down several small saplings so that the entrance of the trail could be seen from a distance of several hundred feet. While he was doing this he looked back constantly for signs of smoke. The new energy that had been surging through his veins a few minutes before was now beginning to wane. The sun was rapidly disappearing and a haze hung over the campo.

"I've got about an hour and a half before dark," he groaned exhaustedly. "If I could see a signal, I could still make it."

Again he scanned the horizon. "There it is!" he shouted. "There it is! Praise the Lord!" The sore spots where the straps had rubbed his shoulders seemed to have vanished and his muscles no longer ached. He had never realized how beautiful smoke looked. Quickly he checked his compass and repeated the direction several times so that he would remember it if he had to come back.

Brian fought his way through the tall grass with compass in hand. Soon he realized he was breathing heavily and slackened his pace. He glanced over his right shoulder and saw that the sun was low in the west. Then he paused a moment. Taking out his revolver, he fired a shot into the air and waited a moment. There it was again—another rocket! Mike—or was it Mr. Weatherton?— had heard his shot and fired off another rocket. He surged forward with new strength. As the light began to fade he strained to see ahead. There it was—the wreckage! He broke into a trot, puffing heavily as perspiration poured off the end of his nose.

"That's Mike," he heard himself say as he drew nearer. Just then Mike saw Brian and came rushing toward him. A few feet from the plane the two met and flung their arms around each other. Brian fought back the tears that began to flood his eyes.

"Man, is it ever good to see you, buddy!" Mike exclaimed.

"I began to wonder if I was going to make it."

"Where's Irwin?" the pilot asked.

"He wrenched his knee two days out and had to go back. I heard later over the radio that he got in O.K. How's Mr. Weatherton?" Brian glanced toward the plane.

"He got banged up quite a bit. I thought he was going to die the second day but he rallied and I believe he'll pull through if we can . . ."

"Can what?" Brian asked.

"I was going to say fly him out, but we don't have anything to clear an airstrip," Mike said with a shrug.

"Maybe we can work something out. What happened to the director?"

"He's got two broken legs and apparently some internal injuries."

"How about yourself?" he asked with concern in his eyes.

"Guess maybe I got a few busted ribs. Got a couple of deep gashes on my leg. If it weren't for the medicine, food and water in the airdrops we'd both be goners in this hot pampa."

Suddenly they both realized they had been talking for some time so they went to the plane. Mike had removed the debris inside the wreckage and had made a comfortable place for Mr. Weatherton to lie. In the fading light Brian could see a thin, haggard man.

"Good to see you, Brian." He spoke weakly as Brian poked his head inside the wrecked plane. "Praise God you made it!"

"I'm . . . I'm sorry to know you got banged up so much, Mr. Weatherton. I'll do my best to get you out as soon as possible so they can get you fixed up." Brian felt deep compassion for the helpless man and realized that he must have suffered much. The raw spots on his shoulders reminded him that he was still carrying his packsack. Mike began to help him struggle out of it but had to stop because of the pain in his ribs.

"Got anything to eat, buddy?" Brian asked as he showed Mike that he had tightened his belt several notches.

"Sure thing. I had a feeling you might be in today so I cooked some extra food. First, let me light a lantern. The Army dropped me a lamp, a little kerosene pressure stove and some good food and whatnot."

Brian dug out his flashlight to help the pilot find his matches and lamp. When the lamp was shining brightly he lit the small kerosene pressure stove to warm the stew. The two men sat on the edge of the wing which had been torn off the plane and was lying several feet from the wreckage.

"Wow, is this grub terrific! Best I've ever tasted."

Mike laughed. "So you like my cooking? It's packaged stuff and all you do is add water and cook it a few minutes. I'm anxious to hear about your trip in."

"You talk first, buddy," Brian said between bites. "I can't wait to hear what happened to you when your radio went out. Tell me first while I eat. I guessed lightning hit you."

"Sure enough. A bolt hit right in front of the windshield while I was talking to you. When I recovered from the blinding flash, my motor had conked out. It must have burned out my electrical system all around. I prepared to coast in for a landing. I knew it was going to be rough because the wind was really strong and gusty. The rain made it nearly impossible to see. Just as I was leveling the plane off, a terrific gust of wind flipped me on my side and we dropped on the right wing. It tore off and we came down with a crash."

Brian served himself the last of the food from the kettle. The pilot reached over and put a small pot of water on the stove for coffee. Then he continued his account.

"I must have been knocked out for a couple of hours. When I came to, I unfastened my safety belt but found my leg was pinned in. I reached down and could feel it was wet. Blood was oozing out. Then I remembered Mr. Weatherton. He was covered with blood and I thought for sure he was dead. I hollered to him, but he didn't respond. Finally I got my leg loose and after I'd cut off the legs of my pants, I tore up my shirt and made a compress for the two deep cuts.

Brian looked up. The yellow gleam of the barn lantern glowed on the faces of the two missionaries. "Did you bleed much?"

"Apparently quite a bit for I sure was weak. I went over to the other side of the plane, which was torn open, as you saw. I finally freed Mr. Weatherton and laid him on the ground. He was still breathing, but unconscious. I stopped his bleeding and sometime in the middle of the night he came to. I was sleeping lightly and heard him groan, asking for water. There was no water so I just tried to comfort him the best I could. He lost more blood than I did but he's picked up quite a bit since we've had food and water dropped to us."

Brian got up stiffly and poured himself a cup of coffee. After taking a swallow, he exclaimed, "Wow, this is the best coffee I've ever had!" Again Mike laughed.

"Now tell me about your trip in."

Brian waited for his coffee to cool. "These aluminum cups sure are no good for hot stuff. I didn't come here just to rescue you fellas. When I can I must talk to Mr. Weatherton about some things that have caused ill feelings in my heart toward him."

"I heard you and June broke up. I imagine our director had something to do with that, judging from some of the remarks made in our council meetings." Mike spoke sympathetically in a low voice that could not be heard by the injured man.

"I don't know for sure. But when he told me he didn't want me to go around with his daughter because of this culture baloney, I figured he would make her believe that I was a good-for-nothing and would eventually influence her to write me that our romance was off." Brian felt a resurgence of the anger he had tried to subdue weeks before. "I've been bitter toward our director because of it and I want to talk with him about it and clear my heart with him."

"I don't know how much of that kind of discussion he can take right now," Mike said, shaking his head. "If he gets upset, it might do damage."

"Pray for me, buddy. There are other things that need clearing up. Guess you know, being on the council, that I'm hanging on a thin thread when it comes to staying in the mission."

"The things I've heard about you, Brian, haven't sounded too good. However, I've often wondered if the whole truth has been told. I've wondered too if Dick and Jim and Roy have a different story. What seems strange to me is that the very suggestions for which you've been criticized are now being carried out."

"Such as?" Brian queried.

"Such as having more men in on the contact, changing locations, carrying guns, and a few more ideas I can't think of right now." Mike turned the lamp a little lower. "I can understand how you felt about the fact that the mission board claimed certain territory but did nothing about evangelizing it." Brian looked up and saw the stars blinking at him.

"Do you suppose Mr. Weatherton was coming out to Panube camp to check up on me?" he asked as he lowered his gaze and rubbed his hand over a five-day beard.

"He mentioned to me that Irwin had changed a lot of his ideas, and I guess the director was pretty worried about that. No doubt he figured you'd brainwashed him to your way of thinking."

"Oh, no." Brian gasped. "I guess I'm really in hot water."

"What's the scoop?" Mike asked.

"I didn't change or brainwash Irwin. I believe the Holy Spirit did a tremendous work of revival in his heart. We are close friends now and he sees almost everything as the rest of us do. We've had real good fellowship lately." Brian sighed deeply.

"How'd it come about?"

"Irwin and I were having clashes about everything. Finally Roy, who is usually quiet, you know, had enough, and told Irwin he'd have been a dead duck if I hadn't saved his life. I . . ."

"*You* saved his life? We never heard anything about that." Mike's eyes opened wide with wonder.

Brian apologized as he related what had happened during the first attack by the savages. He hadn't said anything before, he explained, because he hadn't wanted to boast about his accomplishments. When he was in the hospital he had intended to tell Mr. Weatherton, but just then the doctor had come in angrier than a wounded tiger. Finally, Brian summarized, after Roy had told Irwin what had happened, the assistant director had experienced the shock of his life. "That's when the Lord worked in his heart and things were made right," he concluded.

"Well," Mike exclaimed in surprise, "can you beat that! Things sure are different from what I've heard. Now you've risked your life to help the very man who has nearly destroyed your life. I'm sorry, pal."

"That's all right," Brian heard himself say as he tried to swallow the lump in his throat. "If I hadn't had confidence that eventually God would vindicate that which was right, I'd have called it quits. I nearly did a while back when I got June's letter and then that cable that Mother had died. That was almost more than I could bear."

There were a few minutes of silence. Mike shifted his position as he sat on the piece of wing that was lying on the ground. Brian could see he was deep in thought.

"Too bad he couldn't get in to hear what the other fellas had to say. But then . . . the Lord has allowed this accident for some reason," Brian said resignedly.

"Romans 8:28 is still in the Bible, 'And we know that all things work together for good to them that love God, to them who are the called according to his purpose.' Guess maybe there's a reason for this accident, like you say, but we may not know what it is for a long time, if ever." The pilot got up cautiously.

"Just a minute, Brian. I should go over and check on Mr. Weatherton. I'll be right back."

Brian stood to stretch. He was exhausted but hungered to talk further with Mike. He looked at his luminous watch. It was ten o'clock. The half-moon would rise about midnight. Further thoughts were halted when Mike came back across the flattened grass.

"He's asleep," Mike said as he set the lamp down and again turned it low.

"I was thinking," Brian began, "that if only we could get word out somehow so we could have a shovel and a pickax dropped to us, I'm sure I could have an airstrip cleared in a few days. Did you try to take out the radio to see if it could be fixed?"

"I considered it but I just didn't have any tools to work with. I usually carry emergency tools but the other day one of the national workers cleaned out the plane and forgot to put my tools back in."

"I've got my machete and pocketknife with a screwdriver," Brian said. "Let's see what we can do tomorrow. It's out of the question to try to get Mr. Weatherton out the way I came. If we can't get the radio going, we'll have to think of some other way to get word out."

"Maybe we could clear a spot and spell out "shovel" and "pickax" with pieces of cloth or with strips of aluminum from the plane," the pilot suggested enthusiastically. "If the Army plane comes again, the pilot could read it and maybe catch on."

The men discussed various solutions to their problem. Both of the missionaries were yawning. The piece of moon began to crawl up into the sky, shedding its dull light on the weary men.

"I'm beat," Brian said, slowly straightening himself. "Let's hit the sack. By the way, you got any extra bedding? I left my hammock this morning, covered with fire-ants."

"The Army dropped a couple of air mattresses and blankets. We've also got the front seat of the plane over there. You take my air mattress, since you're longer, and I'll use the seat. O.K.?"

Since there were no mosquitoes in the campo, the two men made their beds under the plane's leaning left wing so that they would be protected from the heavy dew. Brian was deeply grateful that the Lord had enabled him to locate the wreckage and to find both men alive. The only dark cloud on his horizon was the possible result of his conversation with the director. Would he be able to discuss problems with him? Would solutions be reached? These ominous questions threatened the exhausted missionary as sleep overcame him.

CHAPTER THIRTEEN

The eastern sky was just beginning to turn pink when Brian's heavy eyelids opened. He breathed the cool grass-scented air deeply. Quietly he got up and went a few feet to where the other section of the wing lay on the ground. He lit the pressure kerosene stove to heat water for oatmeal. Meanwhile he drew out his New Testament to read. In the stillness of the dawn he praised the Lord and asked Him for wisdom and guidance and strength for the day's tasks.

"Hi, Brian." Mike spoke from behind as he rubbed the sleep from his eyes. "You handsome ole brute. You're a real sight for sore eyes."

"Hi, Mike," he responded, looking over his shoulders. "How's the ribs? Breakfast is ready."

"I feel pretty good as long as I don't bend over or lift anything. I wish I were in better shape to help you."

"Tell you what," Brian said, pumping up the pressure stove so that he could heat water for coffee. "I'll go ahead and eat while you give Mr. Weatherton some breakfast. Then I'll see what I can do to get the radio fixed. I might be able to work out something before our seven-thirty broadcast. With my transistor radio I can hear if we're putting out. I tinkered some with radio sets when I was in high school."

"Sounds good, pal. Go right ahead. If there's anything you think I can help with, just holler," Mike responded, as he filled a bowl with oatmeal for the director.

Brian ate quickly and went over to the plane to greet Mr. Weatherton. Since the radio was nearly concealed by the wreckage, he used his machete to hack away the debris. About half an hour later he laid the radio, transmitter and battery on the surface of the wing. By that time Mike was standing near by, inspecting the equipment.

"Looks like a couple of parts are burned out. Maybe we can improvise. Is your aerial around somewhere?" Brian asked as he connected, cut and rerouted wires.

The sun climbed into the hazy sky and shone upon the tan faces of the men. Beads of heavy dew on the pampa grass sparkled with various colors. Brian tuned his transistor to the mission frequency.

"Let's give it a try, Mike!" he said excitedly as a couple of filament lights came on. Mike spoke into the microphone while his companion moved dials and made adjustments. No sound came. Brian disconnected the plane's radio from the transmitter.

"There seems to be more parts burned out in the radio than in the transmitter so let's try to transmit and listen in on my radio," Brian suggested, working feverishly as Mike helped.

In a few minutes they made the necessary changes and tried again. They could not hear Mike's voice over the radio but when the microphone button was pressed there was a loud squeal. More adjustments were made but still there was only the squealing sound.

"Hey, Brian, I've got an idea!" Mike exclaimed. "In a few minutes it'll be time for our mission broadcast. Let's see if our squealing gets out to Panube camp or the base and if it does, we can use the Morse code to pass on a message."

"Man, that sounds good!" Brian said, looking up with his eyes sparkling. "I don't know if I remember it all, though. It's been several years since I learned Morse code in the Boy Scouts."

"The same for me. I've got a pencil so maybe between the two of us we can figure it out and write it down here on the wing."

The men figured out the code, although there were a few letters they couldn't remember. "The only problem now," Brian added with a tinge of dismay in his voice, "is whether your wife or Roy will catch on to what we're doing and write the code words down."

"Yeah, you've got something there," Mike agreed, rubbing his whiskered chin. "Surely one of those men in Panube camp must have been in the Boy Scouts."

"Let's send an SOS first to get their attention," Brian suggested. "Then we can send a message something like this: 'Send tools for making strip. Mike O.K. Other serious.' "

In a few minutes it was seven-thirty. The men sat anxiously waiting for Mike's wife to call Panube camp. Finally they heard her calling Roy. He answered so Brian started to give long and short signals by pushing in his microphone button. Then they waited and listened.

The feminine voice spoke again. "Roy, you came on clear but then some sort of squealing noise came on and garbled your voice. Please repeat. Over."

"Great stuff!" Mike shouted. "At least we're putting out a strong signal. Let's wait now until Myrna transmits and then we'll send another SOS. Maybe Roy will catch on."

Brian did so and then listened. "Just a minute, Myrna," the men heard Roy say. "That noise sounded like an SOS Morse code signal. Just a minute. Jim has something to say to me. O.K. Jim just had a brainstorm and was wondering if it could be the plane transmitter. I'll give them a call. CP635, is that by any chance you trying to come on? If so, give me three long signals. Over."

Brian fairly jumped for joy as he pressed the button three times.

"That's it! That's it!" the men heard Roy shout. "Apparently you can't send your voice. Jim says you may be trying to send Morse code. Give it a try and we'll write down your longs and shorts and try to decipher them. Over."

Mike stood wringing his hands as Brian slowly sent out the message: "Send tools for making strip. Mike O.K. Other serious."

Roy came back on. "Just a minute. Stand by while Jim tries to figure this out. In the meantime, Myrna, did you pick up the signals? Over."

"Yes, I did, but faintly," Mike's wife answered excitedly. "I can hardly wait to hear what message was sent. Over."

There was silence for a couple of minutes. Then Roy came on again. "We got some of your message. Jim says your signal got weak toward the end and couldn't pick up everything. This is what he got so far. 'Send tools for making.' Then he picked up an s-t-r. We think you said 'strip.' Try again from there on. Over."

Brian tried again to send the rest of the message. "The battery must be going dead," he decided as they began to listen again on the transistor.

Roy came back on. "At the first you came in weakly. We got the letters, *i* and *p*. Then you faded out. Try again. Over."

The men tried again and again but Roy reported that no more signals could be heard. For a few moments, as they kept trying, the faces of the missionaries clouded. Then Mike looked up, beaming. "Well, praise the Lord the battery and set worked long enough to get the most important message out."

The missionaries hugged each other for joy. They also heard Roy tell Myrna that he thought Brian had reached the wreckage. Then they heard Mike's wife reply but her voice quivered with emotion. No doubt she was weeping for joy because now at least there was hope.

"I'll start clearing grass around the plane and then we can set fire to this pampa," Brian said. "That'll save us a lot of work. Maybe this afternoon the Army plane will drop the tools. By that time the fire should be a mile or so away."

"Sounds good," Mike replied. "Sure wish I was able to give you a hand, buddy."

"Don't worry. It's a pleasure to help you men. Let's trust we can get the airstrip made and get you out before the rains begin. The rainy season has been a bit late in starting this year. Once it starts this pampa may flood as most of them do. If it floods before we get the strip finished, brother, we've had it." He shook his head to emphasize the danger.

"I know what you mean, Brian. Most of the pampas I've flown over during the rainy season were flooded. That last storm that brought us down dumped a lot of water."

Brian worked hard cutting the grass in a large area around the plane. Later when he set a match to the matted growth it burned as if ignited by kerosene. The men watched the fire as it roared and crackled. Soon the smoke reddened the sun and caused small whirlwinds. Now they could see plainly the many ant and termite hills which rose three feet above the barren black soil. The two missionaries remarked that they resembled cement tank traps they had seen during the war.

A large cloud formed where the hot smoke pierced the blue sky. The men were happy to see how hungrily the fire ate the dry grass. Mike busied himself preparing dinner and checking with the director. He had propped him up so he could see what was going on. He couldn't sit very long, however, and soon became dizzy and asked to lie down.

A hot breeze accompanied the fire and now and then Brian used his shirt tail to wipe his sweaty brow. Trying to determine the best place to start clearing the surface for the airstrip, he inspected the section which had already been burned. The ground was not entirely level so there were a few humps that would have to be flattened. Before the fire the tall grass had deceptively covered the irregular surface.

Early in the afternoon excitement again ran high as the small single-engined Army plane flew over and dropped a couple of axes, shovels and pickaxes, another rubber "barrel" of water and a few containers of food. The plane dropped the tools and supplies one by one so it had to swoop down half a dozen times.

"Those parachutes sure are beautiful!" Mike exclaimed as the last one billowed open and floated down. After the last chute had dropped, the Army pilot flew low twice. Mike and Brian waved and he soared into the sky, dipping his wings in acknowledgment, and disappeared.

Brian retrieved the tools and other supplies while Mike folded the chutes to ship out later. The sun began to beat furiously upon Brian as he labored the rest of the day hacking at the solid ant and termite houses. He hauled them to the low spots and crushed the chunks of dirt. White eggs and charred insects poured from the channels in the black mounds.

Later, as the two men were eating supper just before dark, Brian said wearily, "If you don't mind, I'm going to hit the sack as soon as it's dark. I'm really beat from that hot sun. I was thinking about walking back to the jungle to take a bath but maybe we can spare a gallon of water for that purpose."

"Sure, go ahead," Mike said thoughtfully. "Nothing better than a bath after a hot, sweaty day."

Brian spoke again between bites of food. "I was thinking of getting up around one o'clock in the morning, when the moon comes up, and doing some more work on the airstrip. Time may be running out on us if the rains begin. I could take a siesta after dinner when it's too hot to work."

"I see your point," the pilot added. "But I sure don't want you to endanger your health by overworking. It wouldn't take much to get a heatstroke or a sunstroke out here."

After bathing, Brian and Mike laid out their bedding as the western sky turned to deep purple just above the horizon. Off to the south the sky glowed orange as the pampa fire continued to burn miles away. Sleep came quickly. Tired and aching, Brian woke as the moon rose above the distant jungle. The air was cool and refreshing as he slipped away a hundred yards to continue his work on the airstrip.

Four more strenuous days came and went. Brian became more and more exhausted and tightened his belt a couple more notches. On the palms of his hands were several blisters. The men had bandaged his sores with strips of cloth torn from one of the parachutes. Antibiotic salve had helped to prevent infection. After an entire day of working in the rain, he feared that he would not be able to rescue the men. If the grassland flooded even a few inches, the water in the jungle would be six to eight feet deep. He had reasoned that he and Mike might be able to swim through the jungle, if they didn't lose their way, but Mr. Weatherton was in no condition to be carried for days on a stretcher.

During the days on the pampa he had felt the need to talk to the director, but when nightfall came he was too exhausted for conversation. "Don't put it off. It may be too late," he heard an inner voice say repeatedly, and Brian determined that the fourth night he would talk to the injured man.

At the end of the fourth day, before dark, Brian asked Mike to inspect the strip to see if he thought it was sufficiently long and level.

"I'm not sure it's long enough for taking off," the pilot said as they walked back together along the strip. "But it's plenty long enough for a landing."

"Maybe we can make the letter o and k out of parachute cloth and the pilot will get the idea it's O.K. to come in. No doubt he'll be over again tomorrow afternoon." Brian walked with his shoulders drooping and his hands in his pockets. "Mike, I gotta talk to Mr. Weatherton tonight."

"Boy, he's pretty weak." Mike shrugged. "I don't know how far you'll get."

"I'd like to have you with me. I won't say much unless he wants to do some talking. If you think it's too hard on him just say so anytime. O.K."

Mike agreed and there was little talk during supper. After they rinsed the dishes the lantern was lit and the two men walked slowly to the plane. Brian suddenly felt all the strength drain from his body. He leaned against the wreckage a few moments to steady himself.

"What's the matter, pal?" he heard Mike ask.

"I feel awfully bushed. I might have overdone it today," he replied, folding his arms above his head and leaning against the side of the wreckage. Shortly the two crawled inside and sat beside the director.

Brian began with a weak, trembling voice. "Mr. Weatherton, I have been wanting to talk with you ever since the last two days of conference. There are a lot of things I'd like to talk about but maybe I should clear one thing from my heart first." He looked at the haggard man. The shadows from the lamp made him look like a corpse.

"Yes, go ahead," the elderly man said with effort.

"First, I . . . I want to tell you I'm sorry I've had real hatred in my heart toward you because of misunderstandings and because I felt you forced June to break up with me." As soon as he said these words he felt as if a heavy burden rolled off his back. Even though he was exhausted, he felt new life surging within him and tingling every nerve.

Mr. Weatherton opened his troubled eyes and then closed them again. A smile crossed his face momentarily. "I'm glad you are finally straightening your heart out. The Lord . . ." He breathed deeply and pain deepened the lines around his mouth and eyes. "The Lord help you to go straight all the way and . . ." He grimaced again.

He still thinks I'm completely in the wrong, Brian thought with dismay. *Well, I've gotten my heart clear and I must guard against further resentment. The Lord will work things out. I . . .* His thoughts were disturbed as he felt Mike's hand on his arm.

He spoke softly to Brian. "Best to leave things as they are." Then he motioned to him to come outside. As he staggered to the battered wing several feet behind the plane, Mike spoke.

"When we get out to the base and he's in better condition, I can explain to him just what has gone on. I'll go to bat for you, pal." Mike spoke reassuringly as he put his arm around Brian. "Keep looking up. Let's hit the sack."

Will Mike have much influence on Mr. Weatherton? Brian wondered as sleep overcame his weary body.

As the morning dawned, the sky was heavy with dark clouds. Waves of despair swept over Brian. Would they get out before the rains started? Myrna radioed the Panube camp for a weather check. Roy reported that it was about the same as that at the pampa. Myrna said it was raining at the base. The Army colonel was in the radio room with Mike's wife and said he would make a rescue attempt immediately.

A slow drizzle was beginning. The men quickly tore four-inch strips from one of the parachutes to make the letters *o* and *k*. As Brian worked it seemed to him extremely unlikely that the plane would make it in. More strips were placed at the far end of the airstrip to show where it terminated. However, about ten o'clock that morning the sound of a motor broke the stillness. Brian tingled with excitement as hope flickered anew. Both of the men took off their T-shirts and waved them frantically as the plane circled overhead.

The Army pilot came in low over the airstrip and then zoomed upward. He lowered his wheels as he circled again.

"He's coming in too fast to land," Mike shouted above the noise. The plane touched the ground and roared back into the air. "Maybe he's testing the firmness of the ground. It's getting slippery, too."

Brian tensed as the plane circled again and the pilot cut his motor and lowered his flaps. "He's making it!" he shouted to Mike. "Praise the Lord!"

The plane taxied over the letters at the end of the strip. "Good morning," the Army colonel said in clear Portuguese. "I almost had to turn back as the weather was lousy a little ways out." He climbed down and the men heartily shook hands and gave each other the Brazilian *abrazo*. "We'd better get going right away as this weather might last several days. How many meters does this airstrip have?"

Mike told him.

"It's a little too short for a full load." He thought for a moment as Brian's countenance clouded. "Hmmmm. That's too bad. The best I can do now is to take your director and Mr. Mike, if that's all right with everyone. I can come back tomorrow morning for you," he said, looking at Brian.

"Fine," Brian said with a touch of disappointment in his voice. "We can't take any chances with this weather getting worse. Let's hurry and get Mr. Weatherton loaded on."

The men carried the director to the Army plane. He groaned and grimaced in pain as they lifted him gently into it. Then Mike turned to Brian. "Man, I hate to leave you in here alone."

"That's all right," Brian assured him. "Praise the Lord that at least you and Mr. Weatherton are getting out now. I'll make out O.K. I'll be praying that you'll have a safe trip in."

The two hugged each other affectionately just before Mike crawled into the plane.

"Until tomorrow," the uniformed pilot said as he shook hands and gave the *abrazo* again.

The plane roared down the runway, using every inch of it before taking to the air. Brian watched until it was out of sight in the heavy mist. A great wave of loneliness swept over the exhausted missionary. It seemed as if a part of his life had left with the plane. He sauntered slowly back to the wreckage and crawled inside to keep dry. In about an hour the rain began to crash down upon the plane. It fell in torrents. There was nothing to do but wait. Hope wavered in his heart. The thoughts of despair disappeared as sleep came upon the weary missionary.

In the afternoon he awoke in time to hear the regular four-thirty mission broadcast. Myrna reported that the plane had arrived and the two men were being treated in the hospital. She also reported that it was raining very hard.

The lone missionary ate a handful of raisins as he didn't want to attempt cooking a meal in the cold rain. As the rain pounded against the wreckage Brian slipped off to sleep once again.

He looked at his watch. It was seven o'clock in the morning. The rain was pelting down mercilessly. He looked out and saw that large puddles were forming around the burned-off campo. "He sure won't make it today," he mumbled dejectedly. "I sure hope it stops before the campo floods."

The situation looked hopeless and his heaviness of heart made it difficult to pray. How deep is the water in the swamp? he wondered.

CHAPTER FOURTEEN

The third morning after the plane left the rain was still falling in torrents. Brian got up and looked across the campo. It was a lake. "Just what I was afraid of," he groaned. "The campo is flooding." He stepped reluctantly into the water to see how deep it was. It covered his ankles. Dejectedly he crawled back inside to think.

If he waited longer, meanwhile the water in the campo would perhaps deepen considerably. Possibly it would be weeks or months before the plane could return. *It's too shallow for pontoons,* he thought. Perhaps the swamp too was impassable now. He would listen to the seven-thirty A.M. mission broadcast before deciding whether to leave or to wait. He wrapped a blanket around his back and shoulders as the wind was blowing through the wreckage. Again he was unable to cook so he ate a small bowl of crushed parched corn and peanuts soaked in water. It was not appetizing but at least it was nutritious.

Finally he tuned in the broadcast. Mike was speaking. ". . . I left the hospital yesterday. The doctors told Mr. Weatherton that he'll have to go to the States as soon as he's able to travel. He was wondering if Irwin could come out, as soon as the weather clears up, to take charge of the work at the base. Over."

Irwin answered. "We had a lot of static so I couldn't read you too clearly but I think I got most of your message. I feel I should wait until we know Brian is out. The way it has been raining here I wouldn't be surprised if the campo might even be flooding. Brian might have to come back the way he went. It's going to be mighty rough. Pray much for him. Over."

"O.K.," Mike continued. "We're praying, and if you're listening, Brian, we want you to know we're pulling for you, buddy. As soon as the weather clears up we'll send the Army plane for you. Do you have anything else, Irwin? Over."

There was little more of interest. Brian looked out and saw that the sky was still heavy with clouds and that there were no indications that the weather would improve. *There's only one possibility left,* he reasoned, *and that's to get going. I hate to think of going back through that miserable swamp and the water will be much deeper besides. Seven or more miserable days are ahead!*

He packed a supply of food in plastic bags and stuffed bedding and an air mattress into the packsack. Adjusting his cap, he stepped out into the rain. Reaching back into the wreckage, he grabbed his gunbelt and fastened it on. As he looked at his compass before heading toward the jungle, he said audibly, "Well, here goes, Lord. I'm looking to You to guide me all the way back. I'll be sunk without Your help."

It was fairly easy to travel the two miles to the jungle, as the grass had been burned off. He found the opening to the trail, and when he had gone only a little way into the dripping jungle the water was already up to his belt. By noon the water was chest-deep and his pack was partially floating. He stopped to eat a few raisins and he knew that farther on the water would be over his head. There was only one way to get through the swamp—swim. *I can't swim loaded down with this pack,* he thought glumly. He had left his heavy shoes behind and was wearing his light tennis shoes. Although he dreaded the thought of parting with the radio, he felt it was necessary to do so. "Lord, I don't like to throw away that which You have supplied, but You know that I can't go on carrying this heavy load."

He relinquished the air mattress and he also took the metal frame off the packsack and tossed it into the water. He must also rid himself of the gunbelt, so after loosening it from the holster, he fastened his gun inside his trousers so it would be anchored securely while he swam. He kept only a few dry clothes, one blanket, a compass, dry cereal, raisins and a piece of nylon cord, all tied securely inside plastic bags. There would be no place in the swamp to lie down to sleep. He would have to find a low branch, tie himself onto it and do his best to catch a few winks of sleep. He was sure that by the end of the trip he would be able to sympathize with the monkeys.

At this point, the blazes on the trees were only about a foot above the clear water, which was chest-deep. How thankful he was for the marks he had made on the trees! How desperate the situation would be if he should be lost in this dismal swamp!

He started out again, slowly feeling his way with his feet. Toward evening the water was up to his neck. He looked around for an easy tree to climb. The rain was still coming down, although it was less severe. All he could hear was the monotonous dripping of the water upon the leaves. A glance at his bluish fingernails confirmed the fact that he was thoroughly chilled. The skin on his hands was wrinkled like that of an old man, particularly in the area, not yet completely healed, which had been severely blistered when he made the airstrip.

Shortly he found a sturdy tree and struggled to the large upper limbs. He selected a spot where the smaller branches forked out and thus afforded him a more comfortable place to rest. A quick survey revealed that the tree was free from ants and termites. Quickly he dug out his dry clothes and blanket and wrapped them in a piece of thin plastic to protect them from the dripping water. Then he fastened the nylon cord around his waist and tied it to a limb near by. This would keep him from falling while he was asleep and thus protect him from broken bones.

He was sure he could endure the night, but could he survive several nights with little sleep? Could he endure a week to ten days of swimming from tree to tree? Just how much could a man endure?

The next six days were filled with misery. Brian pressed on, swimming from tree to tree. He could scarcely see the blazes he had made on the trees as the marks were now two feet below the water. Fortunately, he reflected, the water was clear, or the situation would have been even more desperate. The sky had finally cleared on his third day of traveling through the swamp, and the sight of sunshine had bolstered his spirit. There had been other storms but usually in a couple of hours they had passed.

He didn't take much time to think. His only thoughts were of survival for as each day came and went his strength diminished. At times it seemed as if he could scarcely raise his arms while swimming. His stops to rest, while he held onto shrubs or small trees, became more frequent. Some nights he could scarcely struggle up a tree to endure another night. Several more notches were made in his belt, and, to add to his discomfort, his beard was prickly.

Now and then the thought of June and Mr. Weatherton flashed into his nearly blank mind, but he quickly refused to ponder his past troubles for the present trials were nearly overwhelming.

Finally, on the ninth morning, Brian felt so weak he could scarcely swim. In desperation he struggled out from under his packsack, removed a couple of pounds of raisins, which he slipped inside his shirt, and threw away everything else. Then he took out his revolver and tied it to a tree so that he could perhaps find it later should he or someone else have reason to pass through the area. He then struggled to remove his tennis shoes. He knew that to survive he had to carry as little weight as possible. This was his last hope. Having lightened his load by ten to twelve pounds, he found it easier to swim, even though his arms felt like lead and he had frequent cramps in his legs.

Later in the morning he uttered a weak groan of praise to the Lord as his feet touched the jungle floor. Now and then he pulled out the plastic bag and ate a handful of raisins. Pangs of hunger gnawed at his stomach as he fought on weakly. Gradually the water became more shallow. His hopes began to rise and his spirits revived. Late in the afternoon the water was only knee-deep and Brian made a desperate effort to reach dry ground so that he could lie down and sleep. He was sure he would not be strong enough to climb a tree in which to rest. A glance at his waterproof watch told him he had only an hour before dark. Would he reach dry ground? He panted heavily as he splashed on. Often he fell as his tender feet struck a jagged root.

Finally the ground rose before him. He had reached dry ground! His knees buckled and his mind whirled as he breathed a word of thanks to the Lord before all went blank.

The dawn broke upon the merciless jungle far beyond civilization. Upon its floor lay the exhausted missionary. Mosquitoes devoured him as he slept. The sun rose and filtered its rays through the trees. Brian stirred and thought he heard voices. Had he gone to be with the Lord? Was he hearing the voices of angels? The thought brought a faint smile to his lips. There were the voices again. Someone was touching him. He heard his name. With effort he opened his eyes.

"Brian. Are you all right? Speak to me," he heard the voice say.

He shook his head and focused his eyes. "Irwin! Roy!" He struggled to get up. The two men helped him sit against a tree.

"First let me put some mosquito repellent on you. You're all chewed up!" Roy said as he reached for the small bottle.

"Sure is good to see you men. I must have really slept," Brian said as he looked at his watch. It was a little after ten o'clock.

"We were mightily concerned for you so we started out two days ago to see if we could find you," Irwin explained as he started to dig into his pack. "First let's get a fire going and put on some grub. Man, you're really skin and bones. We figured you'd be heading back as Mike said on the radio that when the weather cleared the Army plane flew back but found the campo flooded and saw no sign of you."

"We figured you should have been back a couple of days ago so when you didn't show up we figured you were having trouble getting through the swamp." Brian could see the compassion in Roy's eyes as he spoke tenderly.

"Trouble isn't the word for it." Brian spoke weakly. "I had to swim for nearly nine days. I should get an Olympics award, don't you think?" He smiled as the bit of humor relieved his tension. A warm feeling of gratitude surged through his every nerve as he watched his companions prepare a welcome meal.

Roy cleared brush and gathered deadwood. Soon the two healthy-looking men had built a fire. "What'll you have, pal?" Irwin asked with mischief in his eyes. "Hamburger and a malted milk or a pizza?"

"I could eat turnips by now and like them," was Brian's quick reply. He then put on a pair of tennis shoes that Roy supplied. They were tight so his friend offered to cut out the toe. Roy, being bigger than Irwin, also gave Brian dry clothing.

He had never fully appreciated the luxury of dry clothes. As he buttoned the shirt he estimated that his weight had dropped to a hundred and forty-five pounds. "Man, if I were my normal hundred and eighty-five pounds, I'd have to hold this shirt together with string."

The men laughed as they found relief from the anxiety they had experienced during the past several days. While the meal was cooking Brian told them all that had happened after he found the plane—how he had succeeded in operating the radio for awhile, how he had made the airstrip, and his other experiences. Often the men shook their heads in sympathy as they heard the moving account.

"That was close," Irwin said. "If that Army plane hadn't gotten in there when it did to take out Mike and Mr. Weatherton, I doubt if the director would have survived the rest of the week."

"How's he doing now?" Brian asked, sipping the hot bouillon that Irwin had given him.

"He's improved enough to travel to the States," Irwin said. "He left with his family the day before we started out to find you. Mike passed word on to us from Mr. Weatherton to tell you he was very sorry about your not being able to be flown out. Also he said to tell you he was praying for you. He said he left a letter for you at the base explaining several things that he had hoped to discuss with you."

"I'm sure curious to know what he's written," Brian said, wrinkling his forehead.

"You're not the only one, pal," Roy inserted. "We all feel that both you and Irwin had better head out to the base for a good rest. His knee has improved but he just doesn't stay off of it long enough for it to heal completely."

"Don't you need us at the contact?" Brian queried, rubbing his bearded face.

"We sure need you," Roy added. "but right now there isn't much danger. The savages have come out again and this time they've brought their wives and children. Their fear seems to be about gone and we've really made progress. They keep asking where Chief Brian is." Brian laughed.

Roy continued. "I guess they figure you're the chief of the white man because you're the strongest, the best-looking and the bravest."

"Come on. Quit feeding me that baloney," Brian admonished, looking suspicious.

"No kidding," Irwin added. "They put the word for chief in front of your name, we figured. Guess they recognize your qualities." Irwin tasted the rice to see if it was done. It was, so he proceeded to open a can of tomato paste and a can of roast beef which he mixed through the rice.

Brian ate heartily and felt considerably stronger. After they had finished drinking their coffee he suggested that they start their journey.

"Are you sure you can make it?" Irwin asked. "If you want to, we can rest a day and leave tomorrow."

"I'm sure I can make it after that long sleep and scrumptious dinner," he said.

The three men proceeded slowly with Brian walking between them. Two days later, in the afternoon, they reached the river.

Immediately the Indians saw them and gathered on the opposite shore. Brian could see Dick and Jim waving excitedly as they prepared to enter the canoe to cross the river. The savages watched as the men embraced on the opposite shore. Shortly as they neared the place where the Indians stood, Brian could see the savages' look of surprise and he observed that each Indian put his hand over his mouth. Slowly the missionary climbed the stairs, stopping halfway to rest.

The jungle people began to wail as he reached the top of the steps. As their wailing increased, Brian asked Dick, "What are they wailing about?"

"I dunno," Dick replied, glancing at the chief. "It sounds like the death wail we heard the other night when a new-born baby died. I'll ask the chief the best I can." He walked the few steps to the brown man and Brian seated himself on the bench against the cabin.

"*Jiwa Ban* [Brian] *chabuna ho.*" "*Jiwa Ban chabuna ho,*" Brian heard the chief repeat over and over. Then Dick came back.

"I think he's saying that Chief Brian is going to die. I guess when anyone has lost weight as you have, they figure he must be dying," Dick explained.

"Tell them that in two moons I'll be big and filled out like I used to be," Brian said, smiling at the chief.

Dick tried to convey the message by gestures and a few words which he repeated over and over, but the chief shook his head in dismay. The wailing continued as the Indians walked to their encampment just inside the jungle. During the night Brian could still hear their wailing as he slipped off to sleep between clean sheets on a soft bed.

CHAPTER FIFTEEN

"Let's stay at a low altitude so we can get a good look at the wreckage," Brian suggested to Mike as he and Irwin climbed into the rented plane.

"That's a good idea. I was flying pretty high when I came in so I couldn't see much," the pilot said as he adjusted his seat belt. Soon they were off into the blue sky, dotted with fleecy white clouds. Brian settled back to recall the pleasant experiences of the past two days. How he had enjoyed the delicious meals, the warm fellowship and the clean bed! He would never forget the way in which the Indians were finally convinced he wasn't going to die. His heart had been warmed when the jungle people brought him pieces of roasted meat and thin pancakes made out of crushed yucca roots and Brazil nuts, as if by their many expressions of concern they could keep him from going into the land of the dead. He was thrilled to see that the Indians had affection for the white man. This realization deepened his love for them and stirred a deep desire to return.

In about half an hour they flew over the wreckage and Mike circled twice to lose altitude. When he barely skimmed the water, Brian could see it had risen even higher in the campo. He estimated the water to be at least two feet deep for many of the ant hills were concealed and part of the wreckage was covered.

"Good thing I didn't stay any longer," Brian spoke loudly above the noise of the motor, "or I would have been swimming through the tree tops in the swamp."

"Probably in circles as you couldn't have seen where the trail went," Irwin added. "Good thing the campo on the north side of the river is high or we'd have had a long boat trip ahead of us." The pilot made a steady climb into the cool, refreshing thinner air.

At the mission base that evening the missionaries gathered in the front room for a time of fellowship. The group consisted of Mike and Myrna, Irwin and his wife, and Evelyn. Just before they assembled, Evelyn approached Brian and asked him not to forget to remind her that there was a letter in the office for him from Mr. Weatherton. She had forgotten the keys.

Everyone wanted to hear Brian describe the events which had occurred after Mike and the director had left the wreckage. They listened with intense interest as he related his experiences. Afterwards Mike suggested that they have a time of praise to the Lord for His care and protection and also of prayer for the director in the States.

Later the group gathered in the kitchen for a snack. Brian followed Evelyn and asked, "I was surprised to see you here yet. What's up?"

Eve smiled sweetly. "Mr. Weatherton asked me to stay on and do some secretarial work since June has left. I haven't yet been released from this responsibility."

"I sure appreciated hearing from you and learning of your constant victory in the Lord. Your letters were a real encouragement to me. It was a great help to know you were praying." He studied her radiant face. The lines of distress were gone and her clear cheeks flushed as he spoke to her. The other missionaries had gone into the kitchen.

He opened the door for her and they joined the rest of the group, who were standing around with coffee cups in their hands. When the missionaries were about to leave, Evelyn slipped out and returned later with the letter for Brian. Then she said "good night" to everyone and went out into the darkness. Brian stuffed the letter into his pocket and excused himself as he was extremely tired. Myrna told him to sleep as long as he pleased and to join them for breakfast when he awoke in the morning.

"I don't want you and Mike to spoil me," he said mischievously.

Mike spoke with determination. "We've got to get some bacon on your ribs, buddy—at least a pound a day."

"That won't be hard with your wife's cooking. She's a humdinger."

Myrna gave him a gentle shove and told him to go home and behave himself. As Brian walked across the patio he reflected on the completely changed atmosphere at the base. The fellowship was inspiring and everyone seemed to be happy and rejoicing in the Lord.

Brian sat on the edge of his bed with the letter from Mr. Weatherton in his hands. Should he read it now and perhaps lose sleep over it? Or should he go to bed feeling happy and grateful for the evening's fellowship and then face the day and the letter the next morning? Just before supper Evelyn had given him other mail which had come from the States, but he was too tired to read it so he put it aside and crawled under the mosquito net for the night. Restful sleep came swiftly to the missionary.

It was ten o'clock the next morning when Brian sauntered over to Mike's apartment. From the kitchen Myrna shouted an invitation for him to come in and as he entered he saw Evelyn sitting at the table.

"Hi, you all," Brian said. "Where's Mike?"

"Up in the blue wonders flying again," Myrna replied. "Have a chair and I'll fix you something. Do you like pancakes?"

"Do I!" exclaimed Brian. "I haven't had any in a coon's age." Turning to Evelyn, he asked, "Did the boss give you the day off?"

She chuckled. "No, every morning at ten this is my hangout for a few minutes. I can't resist Myrna's cookies."

"I know what you mean," Brian said, keeping his eyes on Eve. "We had some out on the campo. Only I got a crumby deal."

"What do you mean by that remark?" Myrna asked, whirling around and pretending to hit him on the head with the pancake turner.

Brian threw up his arms in feigned self-defense. "When the pilot dropped the foodstuff your cookies went to crumbs. But they were the best crumbs anyone could ask for. So I'm going to put a new recipe in our jungle-tips book and call it 'Myrna's Crumbs.' "

"Don't you dare!" she returned, trying to look serious. "I see you're back to your old habit of giving me a bad time. You behave or you won't get another cookie or even a crumb."

Brian laughed and said, "O.K. I give up. I'll be good." Then, turning to Eve, he asked, "What else have you been doing besides pounding a typewriter over there in the office?"

As she told of starting visitation and organizing two Bible classes for children, Brian studied her glowing face. Her silken blond hair was held back by a pair of barrettes and fell gently to her shoulders, where it curled slightly. She said she had received a couple of invitations to speak to high-school students and was rejoicing that a couple of the young people had been saved during the past week.

"Where have you been having your Bible classes?" he asked with deepening interest.

"One is held just a couple of blocks off the main plaza and the other one meets at the west end of town. Oh, yes, I forgot to tell you that I have about half a dozen nurses over on Saturday evenings, too."

Brian's eyes opened wide in amazement for he knew that one of the Bible classes was being held in the area claimed by the Brazilian Interior Mission. Why hadn't someone told her about it? Or had changes been made? He would find out later.

"Praise the Lord," Brian said to Eve. "That sounds good."

"Myrna has gone with me a few times and we hope to start a couple more classes," Eve said, preparing to leave. "If you'll all excuse me, I'll get back to work."

"No hurry," Myrna said as she put the third pancake on Brian's plate. "Hang around a little longer."

"Guess maybe I can as I don't have too much to do yet. I'll probably have plenty of work tomorrow after Irwin reads the stack of mail."

"That reminds me," Brian said, "I haven't read Mr. Weatherton's letter and several others. I'd better scoot over shortly."

Brian excused himself and thanked Myrna for the delicious breakfast. Evelyn also stood and prepared to return to the office. Just outside the door Brian stopped for a moment, then asked, "Are you busy tonight?"

"I don't have anything planned. Why?" Evelyn asked, looking surprised.

"Your Bible classes interest me and I have some questions about them," Brian replied, looking into her gentle eyes.

"What if someone tells June that you and I have been seen together?" she asked as her eyes clouded. "I sure wouldn't want to cause any trouble between you two. I heard I did a while back when you helped me."

"Don't worry, Eve," Brian said, looking at the ground, "we're not going together any more."

Eve gasped. "Oh, no. What happened? Oh . . . I'm sorry. I guess it's none of my business. I'm sorry to hear that."

"That's all right," he assured her. "I'll see you tonight. O.K.?"

"O.K.," she replied as they both went their way.

In his room Brian opened Mr. Weatherton's letter and a check fell out of the envelope. It was made out to him for the amount of one hundred and fifty dollars. *What in the world is this for?* he wondered as he hurriedly unfolded what seemed to be a long letter. His jaw dropped and his eyes widened as he began to read.

". . . and it grieves me deeply to leave for the States tomorrow knowing that you may be lost somewhere in that horrible swamp. I'm very sorry the weather changed and you were not able to fly out. I'm leaving with a heavy heart. I had hoped to talk with you before I left. It's difficult to put my disturbing thoughts on paper.

"I've had several long talks with Mike and he told me many things. Brian, how can I say this and cause you to believe me? God has been dealing with my heart during these days here in the hospital and has shown me many things. I see now how wrong I've been in mistrusting you, resenting you, misjudging you and treating you with contempt. Right from the beginning you were zealous to reach souls for Christ and I didn't defend and help you as I should have. Instead, I no doubt dampened your zeal with my views concerning the ethics of missions and my determination to use 'old proven methods.' In reality I was blind, for the 'old methods' were not accomplishing a thing. I was wrong in not encouraging and helping you as a new missionary. I failed you at the beginning. Your honesty and strong Scriptural convictions angered me that day you were typing letters for me while you were recuperating from the arrow wound. You were brave and made a real effort to help me see the fact that I was too busy and consequently was neglecting spiritual things. I saw your point and determined to do something to correct the situation, but I didn't. Because of your attempt to help me spiritually I again resented your zeal, your convictions and the way you were doing things.

"I felt you were increasing disunity back at the Panube camp, whereas, instead, the Lord was using you to develop deeper unity. Mike told me how you sacrificed your life to protect Mr. Gates. I didn't know that was why you got an arrow in your side. Forgive me for not honestly seeking the whole truth.

"I was sure you had brainwashed Mr. Gates when he wrote telling about several changes. I planned to fly in for the purpose of dismissing you from the mission for encouraging rebellion against its principles. Now I realize that I was the one who was wrong. Will you ever forgive me?"

Brian blinked several times to clear the mist from his eyes. He read on.

"Now I don't know if you are dead or alive. Every day I've asked if there was any news of your getting out. You are several days overdue. I can hardly stand the thought of leaving for the States tomorrow not knowing where or how you are. You sacrificed and risked your life for me even though I dealt with you harshly. Do you have room in your heart to forgive me? I'm sorry some of my actions cannot be undone. I'm thinking of June in this connection. How you must have been hurt! Speaking humanly I can understand why you hated me, as you said out on the campo. Even then my heart wasn't forgiving. God has dealt with me and how thankful I am that He has! My tremendous burden has been lifted, even though I'm deeply regretful and sorrowful to leave Brazil without being able to clear my heart with you. I pray to God that you are alive and will one day read this letter. When you do please write me so I'll know you've forgiven me and that you are well. There were so many other things I wanted to discuss with you. Maybe God in His mercy will allow me to come back to Brazil to do so.

"I'm enclosing a check. It is such a small token of gratitude. I would like you to use it to go somewhere for a restful vacation."

Brian laid the letter on the cot and fell to his knees. There was so much for which to thank the Lord. He rejoiced in the realization that God was faithful to defend and vindicate His own and to bring revival to a heart that rebelled against Him.

I wonder if anything will be changed concerning June, he thought. *I wonder.*

CHAPTER SIXTEEN

A soft jungle-scented breeze drifted into the living room where Brian and Evelyn sat facing each other with a Scrabble game between them on a coffee table. The game was progressing slowly as Eve had answered many of his questions. A delicate fragrance of English perfume made him take deep breaths. Her pink dress was crisp and becoming.

Brian spoke softly. "I noticed your initials were at the bottom of the letter from Mr. Weatherton. Quite a letter, wasn't it?"

There was silence for a few moments. Brian watched her as she stared at the game on the coffee table. He could tell that she was not thinking about the next move. Slowly she looked up. He could see sympathy in her eyes as their glances met. "I didn't know you suffered and went through so much. I wondered sometimes why I was often burdened to pray for you. Now I know. In the middle of all of this, June turned against you. How could you take it all?"

"Your prayers and God's faithfulness strengthened me. I admit that more times than one I wondered if the trials and temptations would overcome me," Brian said, admiring her neatly brushed hair.

"Praise God for that verse in Corinthians, 'There hath no temptation taken you but such as is common to man: but God is faithful, who will not suffer you to be tempted above that ye are able; but will with the temptation also make a way to escape, that ye may be able to bear it.' That verse has often encouraged me since I've been stuck here at the base."

"I think I can understand some of the things you went through, too," he replied, realizing that she had probably clashed with the director also.

"My heart is thrilled for Mr. Weatherton," Eve said with a happy smile. "I'm so glad he is again enjoying the joy and peace of the Lord. I'm sure he will find God's sustaining grace to be sufficient for the surgery and recovery period which lie ahead of him in the States. I guess anybody can get into a spiritual rut if he is not careful to walk with the Lord. I know how it goes."

"Guess it's my turn," he said a few moments after Eve had spoken. After making a play he looked up again at the lovely face before him. There was a conflict within him. Her attractiveness and charm made his blood run faster. Still he couldn't get June out of his mind.

He continued. "Did I ever tell you that you remind me of my mother?"

"How's that?" she asked shyly.

"In several ways. You say things in the same way, and your face, from your eyes up, also resembles hers. Mom often felt the burden to pray during the day or even at night and she was faithful to obey that impulse. I've noticed that characteristic in you, too, and I'm sure the Lord will bless and strengthen your inner life as you pray for others. I've often wondered who would take Mom's place in interceding for me. Perhaps the Lord will use you." Brian felt the blood rush to his face as he suddenly realized that what he had said could perhaps be interpreted to imply a future deepening of their friendship.

Eve also blushed and Brian felt even more uncomfortable because of what he had said. He meant what he had said but there was the embarrassing possibility of giving his words a double meaning. *That might be all right, too,* he decided, *for she is such a lovely young lady. But it's too early to be thinking about that.*

"When are you going to take that vacation that Mr. Weatherton so graciously suggested and provided for?" Eve asked, changing the subject.

"Haven't given it a thought yet. Do you know of a good place for a lonely bachelor to go to enjoy himself?" he asked mischievously.

"It wouldn't cost too much to fly west to Peru to see the Inca ruins. A cooler climate in the mountains might be helpful," she suggested.

"Guess maybe I'd better hang around awhile and let Myrna put some fat on my bones first."

Evelyn looked at her watch. "It's time to go over there now for coffee."

"Sounds like a good idea," Brian said, getting up from his chair. "How about finishing this game tomorrow night?"

"O.K., if you promise not to beat me too devastatingly," she said as her eyes sparkled.

Frequently the following month, before the missionaries started arriving for the field conference, Brian and Evelyn played Scrabble in the evenings. On a couple of occasions when it was evening coffeetime both Mike and Myrna suggested that they go instead to the hamburger shop uptown. Brian wondered if they were gently playing Cupid but he didn't mind. He found it a joyous and satisfying experience to be with Eve. Somehow when he was with her, the memories of June began to fade.

During that month he had received a letter from Mr. Weatherton in reply to the one he had written. The director had been told by doctors that he should not return to the field for at least two years. He also mentioned in his letter that during his many weeks in the hospital the Lord had continued to reveal Himself in a thrilling way and had shown him the spiritual weaknesses in his life. He desired to hear again from Brian, he wrote.

As the young missionary recuperated, he felt the Lord working powerfully in his own heart also. Now he read the missionary biographies and other inspiring books he had never found time to enjoy. He was encouraged by his many long talks with Irwin concerning field policy and the expansion of the work so that other tribes could be reached. Often Irwin sought his opinion and counsel. He enjoyed the walks to the plaza to witness and hand out tracts.

Evelyn was often in his mind. Was he falling in love with her? Could he fall in love again only a few months after his previous romance had crashed miserably on the rocks? He had never experienced a feeling like this. There was confusion in his heart.

Finally the first day of the field conference arrived. There was much speculation regarding possible developments and the outcome of the conference, for this would be the first time in many years that Mr. Weatherton would not be present.

At the first business meeting Irwin announced that he had just received a letter from the home office. He reported that Mr. Weatherton had been asked to serve on the home staff. Therefore during the conference the field council was to appoint a new director, as well as an assistant, to be approved by the missionaries.

"I ask that you folk be much in prayer these days as we meet together as a field council, that the Lord will give us wisdom in presenting to you God's man for the job. There are several matters of field business to discuss and I feel you missionaries should have much to say concerning them." While Irwin spoke, Brian marveled that field business would now be discussed by all the missionaries on the field. This was a tremendous change from the dictatorial policy which had always characterized the mission.

The main speaker, who was to come from the States, was unable to appear because of illness, so Irwin had asked Brian if he would bring a message each day. Two other missionaries also spoke. Brian's heart was thrilled by the singing, the fellowship and the way in which the Lord was working in the heart of each missionary. This was what he had dreamed about in Viet Nam.

On the sixth day of the conference Irwin spoke again at the business meeting. "We have already been discussing and praying about the possibility of branching out and reaching the many tribes here in Brazil that have never had a chance to hear about Jesus Christ. We praise the Lord that He sent Brian to give us the vision and to inspire us to do something about it. We realize that our field has been in a rut for several years. We haven't expanded nor have we added many new missionaries. We have been challenged to make preparations to reach the six tribes that are fairly near us and then to look beyond these tribes to reach many others. We have also considered printing a field paper to send to friends back home. We'll talk about that later. We also have in mind various ways of presenting the missionary challenge so that we will get more recruits to reach these tribes. Therefore, to accomplish these tasks ahead of us, the field council has unanimously agreed to present to you for your approval the following; for field director, Irwin Gates; for assistant director, Brian Allmand; for additional council members, Jim Iverson and Dick Standway."

There was a low murmur throughout the chapel. Irwin began to speak again. "We of the council have thoroughly scrutinized these men's lives to make sure they meet the requirements given in the third chapter of First Timothy. These men have proven themselves. Everyone has highly recommended Brian as my assistant in this work. I believe he is God's man for the job. Let's pass out the paper so you can indicate your approval or disapproval."

Brian was embarrassed as he was given a piece of paper on which to write his vote. *Surely,* he thought, *the field council doesn't know all about my inner life. Have they been talking about what has happened during the past two years?* Maybe the others knew more about him than he realized they did. He folded the slip of paper and put it in his pocket.

The votes were counted and there was a complete one-hundred-per-cent approval of the field council's choice. The congregation began to sing the hymn "Praise God, from Whom All Blessings Flow."

After the meeting that night Evelyn was the first to express her gratitude for the way in which the Lord had worked in the mission and made possible many much-needed changes. She was most grateful, she said sincerely, for the working of the Lord in providing Brian as assistant director.

"Thanks, Eve," he said humbly. "I just can't figure it all out. There are other men more capable. By the way, are you free for awhile?"

"Sure," she said, looking up into his face. "Why?"

"Mind going for a walk?"

"I'd love to."

The night was warm and balmy as the two started toward the river. Under the canopy of sparkling stars Brian took Evelyn's hand. A thrill surged through his veins as she tightened her small hand in his. Neither spoke. Their hands expressed what was in their hearts.

They reached the river bank. A few dimly lit boats were in the port downriver a little way. He turned and faced her. "Eve, I want to tell you something I haven't dared to say for quite sometime, but I have to say it now for I'm sure of my heart."

"What is it, Brian?" she whispered.

Brian could see the reflection of one of the bright stars in her eyes. "I love you, darling. I want you to be my helpmate in accomplishing this tremendous task of reaching tribes for Christ." He drew her close. "Let's use Mr. Weatherton's gift for our honeymoon."

"Darling, for a long time I've wondered in my heart if we were not meant for one another, but I had to keep it a secret. Now the Lord has revealed His will."

Before she could speak further their lips touched as a confirmation of their love and desire to labor together to make Christ known.